The Dress

"A Reflection in Time"

This book...is dedicated to all of those who were told they cannot do something. A fourth grade teacher informed me once, *"That I couldn't put two sentences together to save my life."* Well, I did put "two" together. In fact, I put numerous sentences together, and I called it, **The Dress**.

The Dress
By: Gail J. Kueker

ISBN: 978-0-578-63645-0

Contents

Chapter One:
The Hunt

March tended to be one the most difficult months in Chicago; cold, dreary and still getting dark much too early. It was never quite warm enough to go out without a coat and worse yet, often accompanied with trace amounts of "gray" snow on the ground. Depending on how heavy the snowfall had been that season.

Dallas and Alex, short for Alexandria, needed to brave that weather to buy a new dress for a dance at their high school.

Dallas desired something unique, her vibe, very Boho/Coachella-chic. Alex, on the other hand, was the exact opposite; she is more classic, all things that represent a more refined taste. Dallas and Alex were the best of friends, even when they weren't together physically-they stayed connected by texting or "snapchatting" constantly.

Even though they're inseparable they each had a very different way of looking at the world. Maybe that's why their connection became so strong, they each had a strength in areas that the other does not. Alex was studious, quiet, taking to life safe, easy and methodically. Dallas as an artist, lived just how she liked to paint; bold, intense, and completely out-of-the-box.

The hunt was officially now on for a dress. While, Alex really wanted to go to the mall-Dallas did not, so she instantly got a little snappy.

"Alex you already have an idea of what you want and you know where it is. I'm trying to find something a little less 'typical' let's say, so how about we do the mall on the weekend because I would really love to hit some thrift stores. Are you cool with that?"

"No problem I just need to go back and try it on, " Alex replied, "to double check it and make sure that is really the dress I want."

They both worked it out, so Dallas drove towards the part of town that had several thrift stores in close proximity, that way they could hit them all in a row quite quickly. Arriving at the first store Dallas immediately started scouring the racks. The girls were determined not to return home without an option. Alex was instantly a little bored, but trying to look interested and supportive for her friend. Unfortunately, she had little patience for second-hand clothes.

"Alex, I'm going to try these on-let me know what you think...and be honest," Dallas stated.

"Sure....of course."

As Alex stood near the dressing room, she thought that Dallas must have been having a really difficult time in there. She could hear her friend as she grunted and sighed wrestling with the items she chose to try on. Plus, she was just sensing an overall general frustration with the whole eleventh hour desperate search.

"How are doing? Alex asked, "Let me see? Do you like anything?"

"No," Dallas replied while gathering up all the dresses that didn't work out to put them back. "These are just not it. I really don't know what I'm looking for...but I will know when I see it."

The girls quickly moved on to the next location.

"Dallas, why does it have to be from a thrift store? You have your mom's card why don't you get something brand new?" Alex stated.

"I know, I just want it to be different, I'm tired of seeing the same trends on everybody. It just seems that after a while everybody tends to blend together."

So, on to the next location they went...determined!

At the next shop, the girls once again went into divide and conquer mode. Alex took all the racks on the left, not really sure of what she is trying to find and Dallas took the ones on the right.

With an arm-full of different style dresses of all varying degrees, Dallas headed for the dressing area, confident that this shop will have the "one".

As for Alex, she was busy surveying the store's landscape. She actually found this particular shop quite *quaint*. She couldn't help but touch all the different colors and textures of the garments displayed. The owner had a taken a great deal of her time to find just the right pieces of jewelry and the correct accessory item to pair with each item of clothing, creating the most unique collections. Mesmerized, at every turn, something drew Alex in. From the perched peacocks in the corners, multiple and varied sizes of hanging crystal chandeliers, to the art that filled every wall from ceiling to floor. No wonder Dallas loved this place.

Even the dressing rooms themselves were like something one would find in a vintage Parisian salon somewhere buried in avenues of Saint Germain. It was truly enchanting, a reflection of another time.

Alex became so lost in this menagerie she almost completely forgot about Dallas. As she started her journey back to where she'd left Dallas, she was jolted back to reality by once again hearing the sounds of angst and defeat pouring from behind the thin layer of fabric that was providing Dallas the only layer of privacy. When suddenly something caught Alex's eye as she neared.

For some reason, this item suddenly needed her attention. This "item" seems to almost be an afterthought in the shop. Just kind of thrown on a shelf and forgotten about. As though it was there just to fill up shelf space.

But it totally drew Alex in, and as she reached down to retrieve it. Something deep inside her just knew that this was the dress.

Alex checked the size...size 8 that should be perfect for her. She hurried back to the dressing area only to find that Dallas is now fully dressed and once again defeated, frazzled and kind of resembling a wet cat or someone with a severe static cling issues. Hoping to take her mind off her frustration, Alex quickly stated, "Look I found something."

Dallas looked like she was in no mood to even look at another dress. But she knew that she couldn't leave without something. "I have no desire to wrestle with another dress...but let me see it," Dallas grumbled as though she just left a fight ring and not a dressing room.

Alex held the dress up. It was a beautiful emerald green with a huge off the shoulder collar and self-covered buttons down the front.

Dallas's eyes lit up, and she even managed to squeak out, "I think this might have some potential. I will take it, but let's ask what her return policy is just in case."

Dallas and Alex made their way to the register and Dallas instantly inquired about the return policy, while Alex complimented the owner on her shop.

"Thank you for the lovely compliment," the shop owner replied. "As far as returns, seven days with the receipt and the tags must still be on. I hope that you two can stop by again soon. I'm always finding new and interesting things. Like this particular dress you've selected. I don't know if you know anything about this dress, but she was a local designer here in the Chicago area, quite a few years ago. In fact, I even forgot that I had this dress."

The girls just shrugged, more eager to get home than hear any more about the story at that point.

Happy that maybe she'd possibly found the dress, Dallas grabs her bag and they both head for the door and to the parking lot to find Dallas's car.

Dallas made her way back home after dropping Alex off at her parent's house. She stormed through the front door just in time to hear her Dad calling her for dinner. Dallas ran upstairs and threw her newly purchased dress on her make-shift divan which really was more of an over-sized round chaise, then immediately headed back downstairs for dinner. Hunger, at this time, totally overriding any desire to know whether or not the dress...was a keeper.

Chapter Two:
The Dressmaker

F rancine enjoyed the warmth and glow of the sunlight as it poured through the window of the tailor shop of the Dubois' Tailor Shop as she sewed. Located just outside of Chicago in a small town called Hubbard Woods, it was owned and operated by her parents Francois and Noelle Dubois. The shop originated in Paris where Francine was born, but she and her family had become Americans-after fleeing France just before the war in 1939.

She could sit for hours working on the pieces that her parents had assigned her. Francine had learned her craft well from both her *Maman and Papa* (French for Mother and Father). Her *Papa* taught her how to master tailoring and from her *Maman*, she learned dressmaking skills. Even though Francine loved what she did, she savored designing and creating her own dresses more. Francine had dreams of someday having her own *Atelier* (French for studio or salon).

Her desires and visions had caused a restlessness about

her through the years. Though she was always very present in her work, she found herself more and more daydreaming and reflecting on all of the possibilities and opportunities that could be out there for her outside of her parent's shop. Francine was very practical and very aware of her station in life and how it might not allow such a dream to become a reality.

Like most Saturdays at the shop it was very busy; that was exactly how Francine liked it. Not only because the time flew by, but also because Francine loved meeting and waiting on all of the different clients that came and went during the day. They always shared wonderful stories about all of the events that they will attend wearing one of the gowns or newly tailored garments the Dubois' worked on for them. It just thrilled her.

Even more exciting were the opportunities that came to Francine from the years of being there, the one-of-kind dresses she created for her more particular clients. Those who requested pieces by Francine did so because they not only marveled at her talent and keen eye for style, but most importantly her ability to create very unique garments you just couldn't find anywhere.

In fact, more and more clients were discovering Francine's one-of-kind dresses. So much so, that her father stopped assigning her projects because her own seam work became full-time. Francine had gained a strong following of society women in the area and they all wanted that Francine touch.

One of Francine's favorite past times was to walk down the block a bit to the corner drugstore. Francine would stop and chat with some of her neighboring store owner's. She loved the drug store the most. It had something she coveted; fashion magazines. Besides working specifically on her client's desires, Francine loved being inspired by the latest trends from Vogue, such as a flurry of fuller skirts, brought about after the Second World War. The magazines helped inspire her to create something unique and something she would be proud to put her name on.

Whenever Francine received a consignment from a client she would ask some of the basic questions: Where are you going? Is this special occasion in the afternoon or evening? Favorite colors? Anything she could gather to help this particular garment be one of the best pieces they have ever worn.

When Francine worked with clients it was effortless, a complete knowing on what it would take to make a garment lay just right. It was as though Francine went into a trance, and her subconscious just took over, and she never fought it. She knew exactly what would work and what would not for each custom piece she created. Francine would never sketch, she would simply start draping fabric. Her ability to read the client's needs and intuitively know how to create just that right garment, along with her mastery in constructing something that hung beautifully on them, was a powerful combination that just seemed to bring them alive.

The garments themselves downplayed certain aspects while, emphasizing others. The ladies that wore these custom pieces, felt transcended when wearing a Francine original. To them it was like pure magic. The ladies and those that they spoke too about their own experience, became obsessed. Francine loved it when after whatever special event they attended, they needed to stop back in the shop to simply rave about how they felt wearing her gowns.

So what was her magic? Why did her dressmaking skills stand out from the rest? First off, yes Francine was a superior dressmaker, and yes she knew her fabric, and especially how to drape the fabric just so. To her, clients were not mere hangers for her latest creation. The dresses she created weren't wearing them-they were wearing the dress, because the dresses were specifically designed for them.

Her ability to listen and be very observant, predetermining any and all possible outcomes and problems before they happened, set her apart. This was something that many didn't know how or care to do.

Francine would put her own ego aside and really listen to their needs, budget, what they like and didn't like about their figures, and what they liked about the clothes they felt good in. Most designers and artists love to create their own vision's, separate from what their audience requests. And for the consumers desiring recognition at a certain social level or position, they would choose to wear certain particular labels for status. Whether that dress or outfit was right for them or not. They simply wore it because the label was recognized and "they wanted to be recognized".

Chapter Three:
The Appointment

Two sewing machines hammered away in unison as Papa and Francine both worked to finish up the garments that needed to be competed for the day. When Maman suddenly broke that rhythmic sound of pounding metal, as it was being fed it's daily consumption of cloth.

"Francine, quick come here, Mrs. Prentice-Hall is coming," her mother Noelle nervously blurted in her broken English. Mrs. Dubois always got so excited when a big client like Mrs. Prentice-Hall arrived, not only because it meant another good sale, but because it also gave Noelle bragging rights with all of her friends.

Noelle's eagerness and excitement was palpable, but Francine stayed true to concentrating on her project. Amused by her mother's energetic response, Francine's was more a combination of inquisitiveness and quiet confidence. It was another one of Francine's great assets; a total ability to keep centered and low-key.

Francine's keen sense of calm, combined with a wicked

sense of knowing, and of course her beauty, made her a triple threat. Her beauty was classic, but not obvious. She was tall, slender, with short raven hair which she wore in large curls that dusted her shoulders. Her features though fine, were pronounced. She hated her nose, so she tried to play up her eyes and lips instead. Downplay what you don't like and enhance what you do, was Francine's motto.

Many gentlemen suitors stopped in the shop trying to make conversation with Francine. She had no particular interest in them. Of course, her *Maman* and *Papa* wanted her to get married and start a family of her own, but Francine was not in a hurry, she had her own desires.

Plus, she was very particular, she didn't intend to settle with just anyone willing to pay attention to her. She wanted someone who made impression on her, who captured her attention as well as her heart, and Francine was someone who did not impress easily. Though she was always very polite, she just desired meeting someone unique and no run-of-the-mill man would do for her.

Mrs. Prentice-Hall entered the store, an older woman with a figure that always called for a little extra fabric when Francine created something for her. As the door bursts open, accompanying her was a cool breeze and rustling leaves along the ground. Quickly she pushed the door shut and like most customers, instantly commented on the weather.

"My, my, my, it seems like it's getting colder, when will summer ever get here?"

"Good afternoon Mrs. Prentice-Hall, what brings you in today?" questioned Noelle.

"Well, I have come in to talk to Francine," Mrs. Prentice-Hall said, "is she here?"

"Absolutely, let me get her," Noelle hurried to the back of the shop to fetch Francine, babbling all the way, "Francine-Francine."

"*Oui...Mama* I know, I'm coming," Francine stated as she adjusts her dress and hair, pushing through the curtain that divided the back room from the rest of the shop. "Well Hello Mrs. Prentice-Hall, it is so good to see you again, what brings you in on this beautiful morning?" Francine said while trying to catch her breath.

"Good morning Francine, I just popped in to invite you for tea at my home this Friday around 3:00, will you be available?"

As soon as Prentice-Hall blurted out a few words she suddenly shifted direction and headed back towards the door, even though she'd just arrived. She knew full well Francine's answer would be yes. Even if someone did have the audacity to turn down Mrs. Hall, she didn't want to be in their presence if and when they, chose to do it.

Prentice-Hall, bore quite a reputation in the North Shore of Chicago, as being demanding and over-barring, but in general, she really was a good woman with good intentions-she could just be a touch intense.

Her pull and power didn't end at the state line of Illinois, though. Oh no, it extended all the way to the east coast... as in Long Island, New York, where Prentice-Hall has another home. Prentice-Hall's family made their fortune in book publishing.

"So, Francine, I will see you Friday then, at three sharp-I'm looking forward to it, ta-ta!" Prentice-Hall made her declaration while simultaneously waving her hands in the air as if it was some sort of self-celebration of what just occurred. As she thrust the door open, the sound of leaves once again crackled under her feet and followed her out the door. As quick as she arrived, she was gone.

"Well, that was brief and to the point," declared Francine.

"You're going...*oui*?" her mother added quickly...mixing her French and English as always, which is her preferred way of speaking.

Francine knew that she would be going, but found Mrs. Prentice-Hall's invitation a bit brisk and a touch rude. But in polite and powerful company sometimes ill-mannered moments need to be overlooked. As Francine once again returned to the back room she finally answered her mother, "*Oui...oui* of course."

"Oh good...we will need to make you tres chic...for the tea," Maman replied as she hurried around and gathering some desired fabric for a possible new dress.

As Francine proceeded with her work she explained to her papa, "I think that Maman is more excited about me going to Mrs. Prentice-Hall's on Friday, than I am. I wonder what she wants to meet with me about, I mean if it was about a dress why couldn't we discuss it here in the shop? Oh well, it will be interesting, to say the least."

Chapter Four: The Boy

Dallas and Alex were planning on meeting up after class to talk about the dance and of course anything else that transpired during the last 60 minutes that had not already been texted about between them.

Alex spotted Dallas in the school courtyard and immediately headed in her direction when the guy that Alex likes and was currently seeing, stops her, "Hey how's it going?"

"Hey, great Josh."

Josh tells Alex, "Let me know what's all going down for the dance so I can start arranging things."

Alex was all smiles, very excited as she responds to Josh, "Sure let's talk next week when I have more details of who's all going."

Josh leans in, gives Alex a quick kiss on the lips, and states that he'd talk to her later.

Alex practically skipped towards Dallas afterward,

and as soon as she was within about 5 feet of Dallas, Alex immediately launched into overdrive of how cute Josh is. "Oh, my gosh Josh...he is the hottest. Don't you just love the way he dresses?"

"Yeah, yeah, cute," responds Dallas kind of snarky.

"What's with the tone?" Alex snaps back.

"No tone-just a little frustrated because I just wish that Zach would just ask me already."

Alex looks at Dallas, trying to contain the urge not to roll her eyes "Girl please, if you want to go with him then just ask him." Oops, too late, the eye roll happened anyway.

Dallas and Alex walked off to the school's parking lot to find Dallas's car, so they could go over to her house and hang out. They both were very quiet on the ride to Dallas' home, and as they turned down her street, Alex was once again reminded of the beauty and grandeur of Dallas's home. Her family lived comfortably, but not this comfortable.

They both jumped out of the Jeep at the same time, Dallas then pushed her way through the large wood front door of the home. As they both entered the home they could hear the housekeeper vacuuming in the back of the home, but otherwise they were the only ones home. As the sound of "hello" echoed off the walls. They both grabbed some food from the kitchen and ran up the stairs, ascending them two at a time until they landed in their favorite place of all in the home.

Alex deep in into thought while Dallas finished off the last bit of her apple. Even though Dallas had her own bedroom it was really the attic, an area that was originally used for storage, that they both loved. They both nicknamed it the "hideaway." Dallas was especially proud it because she got to use her own creative flair in creating the environment. Her mom let her do whatever she wanted with the space because it was out of sight from any arriving guests. So, Dallas strung lights from the ceiling and hung a bunch of old art from floor to ceiling that'd been collected by the family for decades. It was a true Bohemian delight.

In the summer the attic got a little hot and in the winter really cold, but autumns and springs were perfect, they could disappear for hours up there.

Another thing that they totally loved was the lake view from the fantastic half-round eight-foot window. So, Dallas purposely positioned her make-shift divan, which was basically an over-sized round chaise in direct alignment with the window. So, no matter if someone was laying down or sitting up, they would always have a panoramic view of the lake.

When Dallas and her family went to Morocco, she was

completely enthralled and inspired by everything that she saw there. It was soon after that trip that her "secret room" had really started to take shape.

"So...how are we going to remedy my problem with Zach?" Dallas asked, as though giving marching orders to Alex.

"Well...like I said, either ask him or don't, this really is a no-brainer," Alex snapped right back.

"Okay, but you know that I prefer things to happen more organically. I feel okay with initiating a conversation, but I would prefer he be the one that actually states it," Dallas said, locked in debate with own desires.

Alex leaned back and found a sweet spot to settle into among the mixed match selection of unique fabrics and textiles, that Dallas found buried throughout the attic. The fabrics surrounding her looked as though they have been custom created for the space. As they were all so carefully selected, wrapped, and tucked to form a sitting area close to the ground near the huge window. The pillows like the divan were a mismatched vision, with its mix of shapes and sizes, beads, and fringe. It was a mass collection of deep rich colors and textures.

"Okay...what you're saying is that you want this to come off naturally, but planned, is that right?" Alex repeated, with a sarcastic edge to her tone.

"Yes, Alex," Dallas quickly sniped back.

"Okay, how about this...I will get Josh to ask Zach if he is going. If he is, then we will know right away. And we can adjust the plan from there. If he is not, I will have Zach say...'then why don't you come with us'?"

"Actually I really like that, but I really want to go with him, not just be a part of the group that he happens to be in."

"Okay, next thought...how about we still have Josh ask Zach and get the basics. Then you can approach him, and say, 'hey I hear you're going to the dance, do you want to hang out together?' What do you think about that?"

"Omigod, I love it! You're the best! See, I knew you would come up with a great answer!"

With that, they quickly settled in and started on their homework both feeling quite confident that their plan of action just might work.

Chapter Five:
The Tea

Francine and her mother were putting the finishing touches on her new dress, the night before the tea. As her mother pulled the last stitch, she insisted Francine try the dress on, "Hurry, go, try it on."

Francine slipped into the very small space allocated as the dressing room for the shop's clients, to slip into the new creation. As Francine carefully pulled the dress over her head, it fell perfectly upon her slender hips, and because there was no mirror, Francine immediately sauntered out of the dressing area, and spun around, and gleefully stated, "Maman, it's perfect for the tea." The dress was beautiful, made from the palest shade of yellow linen with tiny coral flowers all tied together with a delicate white collar, the fell just below her knees.

Mrs. Dubois was ecstatic, raising her arms in a silent cheer, then clasping her hands together while lacing her fingers, almost like a prayer of thanks. She had no doubt her daughter would make a great impression.

Friday morning finally arrived, and as Francine dressed

for work, she knew that she would be taking her new dress with to work so that she could change later in order to feel more refreshed and polished before her meeting.

As the day progressed Francine was starting to feel a little nervous and really couldn't understand why? *I have worked with her before...so why is my stomach in knots?* Francine tried not to pay to much attention to it, and just went about her day at the shop. The time flew by. It was 2 o'clock when Francine realized she needed to change so she could leave.

Francine said good-bye to her parents and made her way down the sidewalk knowing that she would be taking the streetcar to Mrs. Prentice-Hall's home. Her parents needed the car today, so even though taking the street car was noisy, it really was the only practical way of getting to her home.

As the streetcar approached the closest intersection to Prentice-Hall's home, Francine proceed to exit, she knew she had just a short walk up the street after that. When she finally arrived at the address, Francine double-checked the address again, because she could not believe how large the home was. Plus, she wanted to reassure herself that she had the numbers correct and that she was the right place. She knew of the Prentice-Hall's wealth, but this was beyond her imagination.

As Francine pushed open the large iron walking path

gate, she was immediately taken aback by the beauty and sheer perfection of it all. The hedges were immaculately pruned, the walkways were a kaleidoscope of flowers and ground cover. The ivy crawled up the sides of the magnificent structure, winding and twisting as though it was searching for that perfect place to rest. Once Francine reached the dramatic front staircase with its double door entry. She scaled the stairs one by one. Suddenly, she realized that she was no longer nervous, and with that very pleasant recognition, she pressed the doorbell.

The maid had answered within moments. She, of course expected Francine's arrival so she asked her to please step in and she escorted her to the back of the home, to the garden room. Bathed in light, the room was not only warm and inviting it was astonishing. The floor to ceiling windows filled her eyes with one spectacular panoramic view of Lake Michigan.

No matter the power of the Prentice-Hall mansion, Lake Michigan was it's mistress with it's vibrancy and color that carries a resonance of dualities. Appearing calm and tranquil to the naked eye and buried beneath that tranquility, lays it's real secrets. Secret's of the number of lives it has taken from swimmers to pilots practicing take-offs and landings at Navy Pier during the war years. To, of course ship captains trying to navigate it's uncertain and temperamental waters. Lake Michigan has a voracious appetite of unforgiving coldness, undertow and current.

She could easily see why this room is referred to as the garden room as well. The lushness of plants in every conceivable color and state of bloom was almost too much to take in. A seductive aroma cascaded throughout the space. Francine was literally awestruck, rendered speechless by the experience as she worked her way over to the table where Mrs. Prentice-Hall sat, enjoying her tea while she awaited her.

Prentice-Hall stood to greet her warmly with a handshake as Francine approached the table, and asked Francine to join her. The table was set beautifully; the finest china, monogrammed linens and the centerpiece filled with flowers and fruits. Would the beauty never end?

Both ladies took a seat.

"My child," Prentice-Hall said, "I'm so glad that you were able to join me today," Francine, was so visually involved with everything around her, that she barely squeaked out,"Absolutely-my pleasure, your home is so truly spectacular and the view...simply stunning!"

Prentice-Hall went on to explain, "Thank you so much... yes we really enjoy this room especially. Well, I'm sure you're wondering why I asked you here today?"

"Yes, I am."

They sat and enjoyed their tea and petit fors as they both exchanged polite conversation, which merged beautifully with all of the other senses that were taken to extremes in that moment. "Well, I have given this a lot of thought and I would really like you to consider my offer. I'm interested in helping you open your own shop," as Mrs. Prentice-Hall shared.

"Mrs. Prentice-Hall, that is one of the most generous offers I have been given, but I'm afraid that I cannot accept it. It's not that I'm not completely taken back by your offer or even the mere fact that I could even be presented with such a situation...I am. But I have no way of paying you back, or guaranteeing anything."

Prentice-Hall was prepared for this of course, so she stated it again, this time with more conviction, "Francine you would not be sitting here if I had not gone over every detail with my husband and our lawyer's. So, I assure you I'm very serious about this and just so we understand each other completely, we know what we are offering."

"Mrs. Prentice-Hall, I just don't know what to say nor how to even answer you. Can I have some time to think about this and discuss it with my parents?"

"Of course my dear, take all the time you need. My offer has no time restriction. But please if were going to be in business together you must start calling me Molly, it's what all of my friends call me," Prentice-Hall proudly proclaimed.

Mrs. Prentice-Hall's mouth moved...but Francine found herself unable to hear full sentences at that time, because she was quite literally in shock.

As they both finished their tea Mrs. Prentice-Hall's rushed demeanor started to set in again, needing to end their meeting. Both rose from their chairs, and as Francine followed Mrs. Prentice-Hall's lead out of the room that changed her life in more ways than one. Francine thanked Molly for the visit, and reminded her that she will take great consideration over everything that they talked about today.

Francine, then retreated back down the grand entry staircase which she'd nervously climbed when she'd first arrived. Weaving her way back through the kaleidoscope of flowers, Francine heard a car door slam shut in the distance. She turned and looked over her shoulder to find a tall handsome gentlemen working his way towards the same stairs she'd just descended. In that moment she forgot all about Molly's incredible offer and the possibilities of a fresh new reality.

Who was that tall specimen of a man? Francine could barely see through the ray's of sunshine. Whomever he was, he'd captured Francine's attention and captivated her with a single glance. She could not help to be curious of what connection he has to Mrs. Prentice-Hall.

The iron gate glided open as she pushed herself back through it, as though it'd somehow lost all of it's weight. Everything seemed lighter and brighter. She could not help but to turn around again to give another quick glance at the mysterious gentleman making his way up stairs, wishing she could have just left a few minutes later, so they might have have been introduced.

She continued on her way when the sound of the bell clanging in the distance from the street car brought Francine back down to the present moment. Quickly jumping on the car, and happy to find an open seat, as she fell back into it, all of the emotions she'd been holding in since her meeting with Mrs. Prentice-Hall overtook her. She placed her head against the glass of the window and silently...tears fell from her eyes. Tears of complete joy!

So emotionally relaxed Francine nearly fell asleep and almost missed her stop. She rose from her seat and stepped down from the platform to the street soundly. Everything felt so different, the colors of her world seemed deeper and richer, and possibly more significant. Why I'm I feeling as though I'm seeing things for the first time? Why is that? She felt as though her feet were barely touching the ground, it was as though she was floating home. Things like this just didn't happen to the Dubois's and it was all very exciting, thrilling but most of all... mesmerizing to think about such a venture.

Chapter Six:
The Approach

The school day had ended and Dallas still had not received word yet from Alex on whether or not "the plan" had been put into action. She checked her phone it seemed that minutes were ticking by like hours.

Dallas decided to text Alex. What's the story?

Alex quickly texted back...Story?

OMG your killing me! Dallas wrote.

Oh! Josh! Alex suddenly gets on track.

Seriously, I'm about to have a brain hemorrhage over here! Dallas responds.

Got it...let me find out!

While Dallas and Alex "text it out," on another part of the school campus Zach spotted Josh and they walked towards each other. The sun was in full force that day, so Josh almost missed that it was Zach at first.

Let's hope that I can line this thing up, Josh thought as he called out. "Hey Zach!"

"Hey...what's up Josh," Zach said.

Josh launched right into it. "Hey, listen a bunch of us are going to the dance...are you thinking about going?"

Zach, already looking a little bored, now seemed a little uncomfortable, "Yeah sure I liked to go...but you're really not might type."

Josh zigs back, "Dude, I've got my date, I was just wondering if you were going, and I wanted to see if you wanted to all go together?"

The guys are now making their way to where Alex and Dallas are. As they talk, Josh texts Alex, Zach is interested in going...no date! Meet us in the courtyard!

Alex quickly checked her phone when it dinged, she reads the text and then starts screaming, "OMG...it's working...Zach wants to go and he doesn't have a date. Come on, let's hurry they're in the courtyard, we need to finish this thing up." Alex practically drags Dallas, while yelling at her, "Come-on Hurry!"

As they finally make it to the courtyard they calm down and try to appear nonchalant.

"Hey guys!" Alex screams and waves to Josh.

Josh then looks up and sees the girls fast approaching and tells Zach, "There's 'my date' now."

Alex greets Josh with a kiss while explaining, "Wow this is a coincidence running to you guys. Hi, Zach."

Zach shyly reply's back..."Hey Alex...hey Dallas."

Nerves rushed through Dallas, but she knew if she didn't spit it out soon she was going to loose her nerve. "Hey Zach, we're all going to the dance why don't you come with us...I would love to hangout with you?" OMG–I did it! Now pause...DO NOT SAY ANYTHING! Wait for it...wait for it!

Zach replies, "Sure sounds good."

Dallas couldn't believe her ears, or her legs. She needed to sit down and quickly. But remained steady in her dialogue desperately trying not to lose it. "Cool we can all go together. Let me know how all of the specifics will play out, and we'll talk soon." With that she eked out one last courageous statement, trying not to sound to strained, "I'll talk to guys later," and with that she left immediately.

Dallas walked away as fast as she could without it looking like she was running. Though proud of herself for doing it, she wanted to get out of there before every part of her started to shut down from the extreme adrenaline rush and the sheer exhaustion that was now taking hold. Dallas exited the courtyard, found a wall and literally threw her back against it for support.

Somehow Dallas found her way back to her car, barely, pouring herself into the front seat as she exhaled in relief while embracing the essence of pure bliss for stepping out of her comfort zone.

Dallas started the car and headed home, her mind floating away somewhere as she drove.

Alex already knew that the plan worked, now Dallas needed to call her other best-friend. So Dallas instructed her Jeep to, "Call Grandpa."

The ringing echoed throughout the vehicle.

"Hello?" He answered after the third ring.

"Hi Grandpa, it's your favorite person."

He immediately start rattling off names, every name but hers.

"Haha, funny. I did it."

"Did what?" Her Grandpa asked.

"I found the courage to ask someone to the dance...kind of."

"What do you mean kind of?"

"Well, we were in a group conversation and I kind of just said, 'hey do you want to hang out at the dance to-gether'?"

"I'm proud of you Dallas."

"Thanks Grandpa, you're one of the first people I want-ed to tell."

"Well, thank you, that makes me feel very special. Do me a favor, if you really like this guy. After the dance, play it cool. Let him come to you. If he doesn't ask you out, or seem interested, that's his loss, then he just doesn't see what we already know."

Dallas arched an eyebrow. "Okay, grandpa that's great advice. But why?"

"You took a chance and let him know that you're interested which is something that takes a lot of courage, and I'm proud of you for that. But in order to create real connection, men and women need to have a little bit mystery and independence. So, let him pursue you too, don't always be an open book. That adds a lot of excitement."

"Okay...not really understanding why you're telling me this but I think I get what you're trying to say. Just be cool, not all intense and needy. And if he's interested, he'll ask me out again, correct?"

"You got it...but I love the way you stated it, so much simpler."

"Thanks Grandpa, I love talking with you."

"And I love talking to you too."

"Okay, thanks for the advice, we'll talk again soon."

"Yes, love you."

"Love you too, bye."

"Bye."

Chapter Seven: Future Designs

In her parent's shop, Francine was busy trying to complete all of her designs for a local fashion show that would be held at a ladies luncheon at the Lake Shore Country Club during the upcoming weekend. With all of the needed work that had to be done, Francine still had not told her parents about the offer from Mrs. Prentice-Hall.

"Maman and Papa, I want to talk later on tonight about an offer that I received."

"Sure," Papa said, still sewing away, "Can't we start talking about it now?"

"Well, okay, Mrs. Prentice-Hall wants to help me open up my own shop."

"*Tres magifique*, oh Francine we're so happy for you." Maman drops her hand sewing to her lap, to give Francine her complete attention.

"Really? You're not mad?" Francine stated in relief.

"Oh my no! Why would you think that? Papa now

jumping into the conversation.

"Because I won't be working here anymore."

"Oh Francine, we understand." Her Papa said warmly. "This is so good. We could never do this for you. We're so happy for you."

Both Papa and Maman go over to hug Francine.

"I'm so glad, I was worried."

Francine's fears dissipated now that she'd finally told them, and she relaxed, excited about what this opportunity had in store for her. The fashion show was happening in days, so that's what must take precedent.

Both her Maman and her Papa helped Francine long into the nights for many nights after their shop closed for the day. Very late on the last night before the show, Francoius, found Francine fast asleep among her silk's, netting and velvet's. He didn't have the heart to wake her, knowing all about working well into the night-if not even all night-to complete an important project. She needed the rest, so he let her sleep.

It was about 4 am when Francine finally woke to the sound of Maman snoring, fast asleep in her chair while her father sewed furiously. The shop was eerily quiet, Francine was not used to being in the shop this late at night. Francine found it quite magical, the stillness of the night and how the light played so differently in the shop.

While the lamps cast a much needed work light, it was the moon's glow that spilled through the windows and onto the work surfaces and floors, creating a soothing luminosity.

Francine rose from her chair, rubbing exhaustion from her eye's. Just as Francine started to move her lips to speak, her father drew his last stitch that was needed to finish up the very last garment.

"Finished...*bon...tres bon*," declared Papa.

Francine couldn't believe it, he had finished them all.

Yes, there were only a few minor details on many of garments that needed to be finished up. But he did it all!

"Oh Papa!" Francine threw her arms around him, almost too tired to show him proper gratitude. But he smiled, knowing that he'd helped his daughter with something that was as important as this project is to her.

They all worked together to clean up the work space, gathering all of the finished garments so they could be easily transported to the fashion show. As Francine carefully removed the last dress from the dress form, a sudden fear rose over her.

Will they like my dresses?

Will they be interested enough to buy them?

Francine's mind raced, realizing that this would be her first collection she would be presenting to the public. Before the client's would come to her, with their desires, and she would mix their desires with her vision. But now, for the first time these gowns are completely her own design, before the opening of her studio.

But Francine really didn't have time to continue worrying, mainly because she needed to leave for the country club soon. Francine wanted to arrive early enough so that she could have plenty of time to make sure that everything was ready for the models. Francine had asked some of her girlfriend's to model for her and told them all to be there by 11:00 am sharp, allowing them plenty of time to get ready, just in case of last minute touch ups.

Francine gathered up the last of her dresses, with feathers flying and the sequins scratching, she helped her papa load the car to take everything over to the country club. But, first papa wanted to drop Francine home so that they both can rest and freshen up for the very big day ahead.

Francine's nerves raged as they set off for the country club. The drive was a short one, but it really didn't matter because her attention was elsewhere. Even though her eye's were directed towards the side passenger's window, they remained unfocused. The drive passed in what felt like seconds, when suddenly Francine noticed that Papa was pulling the car up to the side entrance of the country club. Quickly they both unloaded the car and made their way to a designated changing area where the models were waiting. All of Francine's friends were there, busy catching up on the things happening in their lives and gossiping about life. Francine started handing out the dresses that they would wear, each one prettier than the other. The girls oohed and ahhed as the dresses were distributed. They had done their own hair and make-up already, so all they needed to do was change into their dresses.

The room became a flurry of netting, gloves, red lips, and chatter. Francine was so busy she even forgot she was supposed to be a nervous wreck. The woman in-charge of the luncheon now approached Francine, "Since I will also be acting as the emcee, I would love to know any specifics that you would like me to feature about your garments," stated the host.

"Has Mrs. Prentice-Hall arrived yet?" Francine interjected, as though she hadn't heard her question.

"Oh yes," The host replied. "Front and center, will you be able to start in about 5 minutes?"

"Five minutes??? Well okay." Hesitation rang in Francine's tone as she stepped away to touch every outfit, double checking to see if all was okay.

The host took her position behind the podium, as the emcee. Plates and silverware clanged rheumatically, along with a melodic hum of talking. "Ladies, ladies...

please quiet down," she said clapping her hands together, shifting their attention towards the front of the room. "We would we like to start the presentation now."

The host cleared her throat before she began.

"As you know we're featuring a new designer to our area and I think that you will just love her and her dresses. In fact, some of you may already know of her talent, and possibly have already had a dress created by her. I know that I have, and when you put on one of Francine's dresses, you find it hard to go back to other designers."

The host continues her introduction, "She originates from Paris, the epitome of good taste, talent that I feel we should embrace now that our country is moving forward after so many difficult years of sadness and war our countries have been embroiled in. So, Miss Dubois has kindly agreed to show us her new collection and she will be featuring her specialty...evening wear."

The host announced the first ensemble, concentrating on all of the aspects that Francine has requested. Then the next one followed, and then another. Soon, all 25 of Francine's finest designs have now finished up their *grande promenade.*

All of the models are now gathered back behind the curtain, and Francine suddenly realized that the audience had fallen silent. Francine peeked her head out of the curtain...and the moment her head popped through the fabric - a thunderous explosion of clapping erupts from the crowd.

Not just clapping, they were standing and cheering for Francine. Francine emerged, so overjoyed, that she had to fight back tears.

She took it all in...and was completely overwhelmed from the outpouring of acceptance.

Chapter Eight:
My Home... In My Home

Dallas barreled her way through the front door of her family's home...and as she screams "HELLO" she immediately runs up the stairs, to her bohemian hideaway, her home, her oasis.

Dallas pushed the door open to her private sanctuary threw her books down on the makeshift chaise lounge, then proceeded to leave back out the same door she arrived. First to use the bathroom, and then to run downstairs to grab some food. She returned to her hide-away within five minutes top.

As Dallas settled into her huge, lush lounge cushions she quickly texted Alex.

OMG....I did it!

I know, Alex replied, I was there!

Oh, yeah! Sorry...just so excited and so out of my body!

No worries...r u home?

Yes!

I'll stop by in 30?

OK!

Dallas cracked open one of her school books and really tried to concentrate. As minutes tick by like hours she found herself exhausted. Snuggled into her cozy place, with a full stomach, her eye's grew heavier and heavier, the book slid from her lap and with a soft thud it hit the floor. Dallas was out.

The sun was making it's way towards the horizon as they both leave the cafe. Evidence of this is the shadow play on the ground, getting longer and more pronounced as day sets into eve.

She doesn't know what is stronger, the rays from the setting sun or the joy and bliss of the essence of us just being together. They had just arrived in Croatia, from Morocco, on their honeymoon.

Loving every single moment, and still basking in the beauty of the memories of Marrakesh. They find themselves constantly entrenched in the colors, smells, and textures of that visual splendor. It was as they were teleported to another time...somewhere completely different then of our current day.

Weaving through the old streets of Hvar, when they finally arrived back at the hotel, full from devouring both an intoxicating meal and from the splendor of love surrounding them, as they stole kisses rounding every tight corridor of the historic and charming place.

The door flew open...as they both landed on the bed. With that impact the sound of falling metal pierces their ears...and breaks the spell of the magnetic connection.

Alex bolted through the door and just as she was about to shout HEY...she noticed that Dallas was stirring in her divan cocoon, "Were you sleeping?"

"Hey...Alex," Dallas said rubbing her eye's. "Yeah, I just had the craziest dream that I was married to Zach and we were on our honeymoon," as Dallas stretches and tries to wake-up.

"Are you serious? Wow...you're really crazy about this guy."

"Well, yeah, but I didn't try to plan my dream it just played out...in my head." Snaps Dallas!

"Got it. Well how much homework do you have?" Alex asked, quickly changing the subject.

"Not much...just trying to get through these chapters... for a test tomorrow," Dallas said through a yawn.

"You know, did you ever try that dress on that we found at that vintage store in town?" Alex asked Dallas.

"No...in fact I completely forgot about it." Dallas shot to her feet, started rummaging around her space completely forgetting about how tired she'd been just a second ago. Literally tearing up the blankets, the pillows go flying everywhere, the string of lights swayed from the impact of being hit with the flying pillows. Shear panic sets in as Dallas has ensued a full on rescue mission to locate the dress.

After literally destroying her abode, Dallas shrieks, "AH HA!" One dress...in a bag...found!"

Dallas tore into the bag to retrieve the dress, going from ecstasy of discovering the dress, to total shock and complete stillness standing in the reality of the fact that she hasn't even tried the dress on yet.

She hurried over to the folding screen that she tucked into the corner of room. The attic, or now commonly known as Dallas's Bohemian Hideaway, became the mecca of all things collected and gathered. Dallas darted behind the screen, to remove her current clothes throwing them over the top of the screen. She slipped the dress over her head, and it slid perfectly over her hips. "Awesome!" Dallas shouted as she walked around to the other side of the screen.

Alex leaped off the divan and knocks all of her books onto the floor. As she got up, she approached Dallas to see what the dress looked like up close. With total sincerity Alex states, "Wow, that really looks good on you! I checked the size when I first saw that dress sitting on the shelf, but I had no idea how perfect and beautiful that dress would be on you. I literally was just following a gut feeling that you needed to try it on.

Dallas now ran over to the dressing mirror positioned next to her folding screen. As she took in the reflection she too is kind of shocked about how well the dress fit her. The bias cut gown laid perfectly across her hips.

Dallas twirl's around and proclaims, "I think Zach...is going to find it hard to take his eye's off of me at the dance."

"I think you're right," Alex quickly agrees.

"Okay, so major crisis diverted, dress fits,"

"Now we have all of the needed elements in place. The dress and the date...the rest is up to the universe," Dallas proudly proclaims.

Alex nodded, "Agreed!"

"I wonder, what the night will bring?" Dallas questioned.

"I don't know, but I'm sure we will all have a good time." Alex replied.

Chapter Nine:
At First Glance!

The chatter coming from the ladies that now surrounded Francine as they pushed their way through the back curtain to congratulate her, was overwhelming to Francine. The sound instantly became muffled, Francine had now completely disconnected herself from everything that was going on around her.

Shock, perhaps? Disbelief? Even though she was physically moving, and gathering all of her new creations from the makeshift changing area, emotionally she'd completely zoned-out. Shocked into silence after what'd just occurred with the standing ovation. The show had been a huge success, and now Francine was numb, so taken back by the reception and vast approval of all of her designs.

As Francine and her Papa finished loading the car back up, she struggled to focus back on the present moment. Eventually she decided to stop arguing with herself and agreed that this experience along with the offer from Mrs. Prentice-Hall was something extraordinary, and she would just enjoy the bliss of it.

As they drove back to the shop, Francine came back into her body, on the verge of tears; so much emotion flooding through her. Papa parked the car at the back of the store and jumped out to start unloading, clueless to the tears flowing down Francine's cheeks as he raises the lid to the trunk.

The squeak from the lifting the trunk's lid was ever present, no matter how many times Papa oiled the hinges-it forced Francine's thoughts back to the car and to the fact that she needed to help her papa. He'd never stopped, nor complained, though he'd worked all night and supported her to see her visions come to life.

Her gloved hand wiped away her tears, Francine needed to collect herself and get out of the car to help him unload. As Francine finished carrying in the last armful of dresses, she immediately headed for the closest chair to flop down in. When suddenly, the bell on the shop door rang, just as Francine was starting to relax. A sound that pierced through the exhaustion, of her body and mind, both of which are aching to sleep.

Because Papa was still out back returning things to the shop that were used in the fashion show, and Francine didn't really know where her Maman was.

The only thing separating her from the front of the shop was a thin curtain. That curtain was used to hide a multitude of sins in the back of the shop, such as the numerous garments needing repairs, a peg board filled with every color thread, along with the pressing and sewing machines.

"Hello?" A man's voice called out.

"Hello...is anyone here? The stranger asked.

"Yes...I'm here," replied Francine.

She pushed through the curtains, then froze in her tracks; she couldn't believe who was standing in her shop. Was it him...the man who'd gotten out of the car at Prentice-Hall's home? Or I'm I just that tired, and my mind is playing tricks on me?

He stepped closer as Francine questioned her memory. "Well hello, I remember you," the stranger states with a kind voice.

"You do?"

"Yes, you had lunch at my Aunt's and I was just arriving as you were leaving," the handsome gentlemen states.

"Really?" Francine asked, continuing to play coy.

"Sure, my Aunt asked me to come by to see how the fashion show went. And to ask you to come by the house so that you both can finish up on the needed paperwork for the new shop," stated the gentleman.

"By the way my name is Steven," as he extended his hand to shake Francine's.

"Hi Steven, I'm Francine," she said as she accepted the hand.

Steven walked around the shop, and while he was taking in the inventory, Francine took inventory of Steven: Extremely tall, even more handsome than she remembered, and perhaps a little to confident for his own good.

"My aunt would love to know if you're available next Saturday," Steven stated as he continued to survey the shop, "How does that sound?"

"I would love to come by her home again," Francine said.

"Actually," Steven adds, now that I'm here, I think it would be nicer to meet you for dinner somewhere...perhaps at one of my favorite places, how does that sound?"

"Well, sure." Though she tried, Francine couldn't conceal the hesitation in her voice.

"Great...so next Saturday around 7...and we will pick you up. Why don't you write down your address?"

Steven was very insistent...almost a little over bearing for Francine's taste. While she searched for a blank piece of paper to write her address on, she was part intrigued and part put off. She was sure that he meant well, and knowing that he was connected to Mrs. Prentice-Hall, she needed to be cautious of his intentions.

Their hands brushed slightly as he took the paper, and for a moment, they looked deeply into each other's eyes.

Right there, in that moment all of his false bravado and take charge demeanor, was gone. Francine could now see him, and knew a connection had formed between them. What that connection was all about...she had no idea. All she knew, is that it was there.

Francine retracted her hand, breaking the awkwardness and her awareness quickly with, "You know...after taking a minute to think about it. I think, I will be working all day on Saturday and you never know what the day will be like. So, if you don't mind I would prefer to meet you both at the restaurant."

"Oh sure," Steven said. The restaurant is on the corner of Greenbay Road and Pine, you can't miss it."

"Great...I look forward to it and I will see you both next Saturday at 7 then!" Francine inserted a brusque urgency to her tone, anxious to conclude this intense encounter.

Steven's calm demeanor faltered for just a moment. It was evident that both of them knew that something occurred between them.

Francine walked Steven to the door and as he pulled the door open, he turned back quickly, as though he'd forgotten to say something. Not realizing that Francine was right behind him, he nearly knocked Francine over.

"Oh my gosh...I'm so sorry." Steven grabbed Francine by her fore-arms. Even though the force caught her off guard, the soft gentle grasp of his hands as he tried to protect her from hitting the floor was somehow familiar and very comforting to Francine.

"I'm fine," Francine says, brushing her dress down around her petite frame, trying to find her balance again.

Steven tries to gather himself from the embarrassment and his nervous excitement as he stumbles back towards the doorway. "Okay, well I, we, will see you Saturday evening! Have a great afternoon, Francine."

"Yes, you too, Steven."

The bell chimes as the door slams shut, and Steven heads briskly back towards his car, relieved to be out of the shop and away from Francine. By the time Steven got into his car, he had a major realization that in his haste to put as much distance as he could from him and Francine, which had nothing negative to do with Francine. In fact, for the first time ever, this man was literally brought to his knees by a woman, and that was something that Steven was not used to.

The sound of the bell lingered in Francine's ears as she found her way back to the same chair that was her original target before her life had taken another mysterious turn. Francine cautiously descended onto the chair, as though she was not really sure that the chair would even be there. Francine has a look of complete shock and total excitement at the same time, she knew at first site that

Steven was going to be someone very special in her life.

Francine sat there dissolving into the chair, as she reflected back on Steven's touch and the intensity of his eye's, completely and utterly overwhelmed by the encounters this day has brought, and the potential therein. Her bliss was suddenly interrupted by her Papa crashing through the door carrying the last of the things left that were left in the trunk. Her Maman followed closely behind her papa looking a little guilty.

"Where have you two been?" Francine asked.

"Out back," they responded in unison, then broke into small giggles.

Francine had been surrounded by love her whole life, her parents never shied away from showing their love and affection for each other. By stealing kisses, and dancing close even when there was no music playing. With the exception of a tune from whatever Papa was humming or even the soft sound of his singing.

Francine finally got up from the chair and declared that she was going home. Though they were all exhausted, she knows that her parents would prefer to stay at that shop to clean up and do anything they can to finish up on some last minute garment touches, before they both call it a day. It didn't matter how small the task was, they just liked being in each other's presence, that's what made them the most happy.

Chapter Ten:
Is This a Meeting or a Date?

F rancine ran around her room practically knocking things over trying to get ready for this...meeting?! She knew that she was running late from a long day at the shop. Francine was constantly checking her watch and herself in the mirror, smoothing down her dress, like some kind of nervous twitch.

"Why am I so nervous with the way I look? You would think that I was acting as though this is a date." Francine murmured.

Francine whisked by her parents; her Papa was sitting at the kitchen table, while her Maman was placing the meal that she'd just prepared for him on the table. The soft light of the room cascaded over them so beautifully. The soft lighting combined with transcendent aromas of Maman's cooking, created an incredible ambiance of their love-Francine needed to just take a moment of pause.

Reality forced her back down to the time and the importance of leaving so Francine shouted while running out the door, "I'm leaving...I don't know when I will back, but I'm sure that it won't be too late....love you!"

She scurried down the front steps of the home and wound down the path to the driveway, jumping into the front seat of the family car. Yes, Francine was now physically driving the car but her mind was someplace else; excited and nervous at the same time, focused on the meeting and how the evening would play out. The drive passed in a blink.

Without even realizing it she now pulled in the restaurants' parking lot, and quickly jumped out of the car. In her haste to get inside the restaurant, she caught her skirt in the car door. Francine was already flustered from running late and now this, as she tries to unfurl herself from this precarious position she realized she could not turn around and open the car without tearing her skirt. Teetering between emotions, Francine shrieked, "Oh great, now what do I do?"

Seconds felt like hours, as she stood there checking her watch, scolding herself: *How is knowing the time going to help me out of this jam?* Perhaps subconsciously she knew that she was already late, and she was hoping that time would somehow just stand still. Well, guess what? Now it is!

Then a car pulls into the parking lot-the headlights pierce Francine's eyes-she is temporary blinded. She raised her gloved hand to shade her eyes. The car found a space to pull in, and as soon as the gentlemen got out of the car, Francine immediately called for assistance.

"Excuse me sir, can you please help me?"

As he hastened to her aid, she realized that the gentleman was Steven.

"Francine is that you?" Steve asked.

A mixture of shock, embarrassment, and relief filled Francine, "Yes. Steven oh thank heaven, can you please help me, I have seemed to have gotten my skirt caught in the car door?"

Steven squeezed in the tight space that was available between her and the car parked right next to her. He shifted his body so that he could get between Francine and the car door. Steven excused himself as he brushed up against Francine. Who now was part mortified and part confused about the sudden sensations rushing through her at his nearness.

Once Steven opened the door, and Francine fell into his arms, partly out of excitement of being free, but also because there was literally no space between them. Francine excused herself as she tried to regain her stance.

"We both seem to have problems with doors."

They both laughed, remembering how they both had a difficult moment in a "door way" when they first met at her Papa's shop.

After Francine collected herself, Steven escorted her into the restaurant. They walked up to the door together, as Steven continued to guide her through the beautiful restaurant, following the host, he supported her arm until she was safely at their table. The richness of the colors and textures of all of the fabrics, from the drapes to the tablecloths, Francine was immediately enamored.

As a fashion designer (though Francine would always consider herself a dressmaker) of course those were the first details she noticed as she removed her gloves one finger at a time. Her eye's then immediately went to the fireplace as she enjoyed the coziness and warmth emitting from the flames. Not to mention the magnificent light play that was occurring from the flames' reflection on the walls and floors.

They settled into their assigned table, and Francine emotionally and physically exhaled an awed breath as she turned to Steven and said, "Wow, what wonderful place...do you come here often?"

"Yes, it's one of my favorite places in town." Steven replid. "In fact, after tonight it might have even more of a special meaning."

"Why is that?" Francine asked.

"I've always liked the food and atmosphere here, but now that I have the enjoyment of your company, it makes this an even more of a special location."

Francine blushed, dropped her gaze to her skirt, draped across the seat of the banquette, and noticed that there is a hole in her skirt. Of course she was upset about it, and normally she would have been pretty stressed out that her skirt had been damaged and embarrassed that her "outfit" was ruined. But she is in a completely different head space with Steven, she is more intrigued by the possibilities this night would bring, and in that moment she could have cared less.

"Where is your Aunt?" Francine asked. "I thought that she was joining us too?"

"She wasn't feeling very well, she said to just go ahead on and handle everything without her," Steven explained.

"Oh, well, I hope that she feels better soon," Francine said, adding a note of concern to her tone.

"Yes, thank you I will tell her that you asked about her," Steven smiled, and adjusted nervously in the booth, "What looks good to you on the menu?" As he changes the subject.

As they sat, talked, and dined, enjoying each other's company, the hours flew by. The sound of a soft violin being played in the background, accompanied with the occasional snap and crackle from the firewood as it burned throughout the evening, was the perfect accompaniment to an already magical evening for Francine. These types of evenings were certainly not the norm for her. She realizes this had become something far more than a business dinner, and she didn't have any problem with that, at all.

Steven pulled out some papers from his suit coat, when they moved on to their after dinner drinks. "Well, my Aunt would be very disappointed if I forgot to give you these papers to sign."

"Oh yes...so exciting," stated Francine as she leaned in towards Steven. In fact, she realized that she'd been moving closer and closer to Steven all night long. Francine personally recognized that there was definitely a strong connection between Steven and her. But, she reminded herself why she was there in the first place, and needed to make sure that took precedent.

Steven instructed Francine to have her lawyer look at the papers to see if they were agreeable, so that they could move forward. As Francine placed the papers in her purse, she secretly thought that really any deal was okay. She knew this type of opportunity didn't come around very often...if ever. Either way, Francine would have her Papa review the paper work later.

They sat at their booth for hours, but to them there was no time at all. The waiter and the Maitre d of the restaurant paced back and forth in front of their table, hoping they would get the hint so that they could return home to their own loved ones. Suddenly, Steven brought Francine and himself back to the present moment, connecting to the fact that he needed to pay their bill and leave, because they were the last ones left in the restaurant.

Steven escorted Francine to her car and carefully placed her back into the driver's seat as though she were a fragile package, making sure she didn't catch her skirt on the door a second time. Francine extended her hand for Steven to shake. Steven took Francine's hand in return, and as he received her hand to shake, he turned it over and clasped his hand over hers. Almost like he was trying to shift from "business" mode to a "protective and nurturing" mode. They said their good-bye's, then Francine drove away into the night with an outer glow brighter than the moon.

Chapter Eleven:
A Quick Haircut with
Some Psychic Advice on
the Side, Please!

On the weekend before the dance Dallas texted Alex to see if she wanted to go to the salon for haircut, blow out, possibly a mani and pedi – basically the works! Dallas reached for her phone on the nightstand, as the morning sun poured through the window on a rare gorgeous spring day. Swaddled in her clean white sheets, Dallas was enjoying the fact that she got to sleep in, and was mesmerized by the light show of dust particles floating through the morning sunlight.

Just outside her window the gardener started working on a bed of hydrangea's that her Mom had insisted on being just that perfect shade of blue, for summer. An hour had passed, while enjoying the leisure of a Saturday morning, Dallas figured that the universe was calling for her to start her day. Besides, hunger was now starting to overpower all desire to be hypnotized by the continuous ensemble of dust ballerinas magnified by the sunlight.

Dallas showered and dressed quickly all while intermittently checking her phone for the time and any texts that might have come in from Alex. Dallas decided to text Alex to let her know that she will be at the salon closer to 1 than 12:30. As soon as she hits send, Dallas also realized she'd received a text from Zach. She quickly opened it up, excited to read that Zach had asked about the time and address for him to arrive at her house for the dance. Dallas, decided to play it cool and send him a quick response about how she was running out the door and that she would text him later with details. A girl needed to look like she has a life too-especially when your really crazy about the guy!

Dallas grabbed her key's and yelled to her family, wherever they were in the house, "Bye...home later." Backing her jeep out of the driveway, barreling down the road, loving the feel of sunshine on her face and what life was serving up in that moment.

She soon arrived at the salon and found Alex hanging out in front. Dallas parked and quickly jumped out to meet Alex. The strange thing was, as Dallas approached Alex, she noticed that her face was screwed into an expression of concern from her vantage point.

"What's going on?" Dallas asked. "How come you're out

here?"

"They messed up our appointment time," Alex signed. "They can't get us in for another two hours."

"Are you serious...really?"

The girls parked themselves on the edge of the curb.

"Well...what do you want to do for the next two hours?" Dallas asked.

Alex suggests, "We can go to the mall?" Dallas doesn't respond, which Alex took as a "no".

They hung out for awhile on the edge of the sidewalk. Dallas was taking in the view when she happened to spot a sign that caught her attention across the street. "Hey let's go there!" As Dallas points to this crazy looking house with it's overgrown trees, wildflowers and more garden ornaments then a craft store.

Alex looked up, not really understanding what Dallas was referring too or where she was even pointing, "What?"

"There...across the street...let's go...she's a psychic. Let's go see what she charges," Dallas insisted.

Caught off-guard, Alex was still trying to figure out what Dallas was talking about, as Dallas dragged her across the street, dodging oncoming traffic at the same time. As they approached the door, Dallas reached down and turned the doorknob to push the front door open; a little tough at first, but she managed it. The buzzing neon lights in the window grew louder as Alex followed close behind, almost glued to Dallas's heels. Alex grabbed Dallas's hand as they crept their way in further and further into this business, taking each step in unison at a snail's pace.

"Hello? Dallas called out. "Is there anyone here?"

Even though there was no one in sight, the girls were still taking in every inch of this incredible visual emporium. Dallas first noticed the floor, an inlay of pennies from wall to wall in the entry hall which seemed to constantly change colors from the reflection of the flashing neon sign hanging on the back wall of the shop. The sign, a giant hand with the words PALM READER below it. By the look of the shop, Dallas seemed to have met her match when when it came to creating unique bohemian interiors.

As they walked through the small entrance way, they crept their way into the next room that literally took their breath away, it was filled with candles. They were everywhere! They started from inside and on top of the fireplace, spilling out onto the floor in every direction. All of them were the same shade of cream in various heights and widths. The room was literally glowing. A woman's voice broke their enchantment, it was coming from the far end of that same room. As they both adjusted their vision, they discovered this woman, sitting at a huge table like desk, her chair was more reminiscent of a throne. The chair/throne was in the most beautiful shade of aubergine. In fact, the whole place seemed to be literally draped, in every various shade of violet possible.

The woman asked the girls to come in and to take a seat. They cautiously worked their way over to some chairs positioned in front of her very large table. The gypsy woman was beautiful with her jet-black hair and dark eye's, Dallas thought that she looked a lot like Kat VonD without the tattoos. The gypsy leaned forward in her "throne" and asked the girls, "What brings you both here today?"

Dallas and Alex were still pretty much speechless, but Dallas finally cleared her throat and spoke up, "Well my name is Dallas and this is my friend Alex. We, well me, I was just curious. I kind of dragged my friend Alex in here with me. I don't really understand what you do."

The gypsy woman relaxed back into her chair, "I take it that neither of you had a reading done before?"

"No," Dallas replied, "but I always thought it would be really cool. How much does a reading cost?"

"Well, I can offer you a special of $75.00 for an hour reading? That will give you the choice of me using Tarot cards or a reading of your palm?"

Dallas adjusted herself in her chair, and thought, *Okay now how am I going to explain this charge on my card. Well* *you see Mom...Alex and I walked into this store and this gypsy lady said that she could tell me my future for $75.00. So, guess what? I tried it!*

Yeah...she wouldn't like that explanation at all. As Dallas sat back, her mind buzzing away as she visualized this whole conversation of trying to reconcile that transaction to her Mom. With that vision still in her mind she grabbed her purse and states, "Do you take Visa or American Express for a tarot reading?"

The gypsy sat up and stated, "Both!"

The gypsy took her payment and then she shuffled the deck of cards. When she was done she asked Dallas to think of her question or questions and cut the deck 3 times. Dallas grabbed the deck and cuts it three times, finding it difficult because they were quite large and hard to handle. The gypsy then retrieved the cards and proceeded to place them in some sort of pattern that only made sense to her. With each card placement she took a moment to review the card. When she concluded the layout, she then started to interpret the cards back to Dallas.

"Dallas, I think that you're needing clarification on a particular situation that revolves around love is that correct?"

Dallas's eyes grew wide, "Yes...that's exactly it."

The gypsy continued, "I see that this is something very new."

"Yes", Dallas replied enthralled by everything that is going on around her, from the environment to the actual reading.

Alex on the other hand didn't say much, Dallas assumed, she was just "weirded" out or something. Especially since Dallas noticed that Alex seems to have adopted some sort of nervous tic of looking behind her as though she thought someone was going to sneak up on her.

Dallas was much more interested in studying the gypsy than what was going on with Alex. In fact, Dallas watched the gypsy with such intensity that she was literally on the edge of her chair filled with anticipation of what the gypsy would say next. Dallas watched as the gypsy reviewed the cards, fascinated by how she took her fingers and carefully touched each card.

"Dallas, as I have already said, this new experience that I see for you, it involves a man." The gypsy stated.

"Yes!"

The gypsy continued, "I feel that this new connection is actually a really good one for both of you. This young man seems genuine and interested in knowing more about you and spending time with you. Though I can't see what the outcome of your connection is, I do see happy times spent together...possibly even traveling together. I want you to know that I don't discuss anything really dark...but there is something here in the cards about this particular meeting coming up. Possibly it's a gathering? There is something of a caution, a heavy energy around it...it's not that you will be in danger. But there is something involved with this particular event that carries an unforeseen energy, a sadness...but it's not clear whether this is a person, a situation or an object that creates the sadness."

The gypsy went on to talk about some other things she saw in the cards, but as far as Dallas was concerned she had heard what she wanted to hear-the rest overloaded her senses. Dallas and Alex were starting to show signs of tiring and getting physically antsy, squirming in their seats, looking around and becoming unfocused. The gypsy picked up on this; their time was about up anyways. The gypsy closed the reading, by stating that she hoped that they enjoyed the reading enough so that that they would be back someday. They both got up and started making their way towards the door that they'd entered from.

As Dallas walked out the door she turned to Alex and stated, "So what did you think?"

"Well, it was interesting. The whole thing was just strange...but as long as you liked it,"

"Yes, I did...though the fact she brought up that there will be a some difficult energy around the dance has me freaked out a bit. Even though she didn't say the word 'dance,' we both know that is the major 'gathering' coming up."

Though Alex was still a little freaked out by the whole thing, she tried to console her friend by being sensitive to what was said. "I really think she might have been referring to something outside of your control...maybe the place is haunted or something?"

"Our school gym?" shrieked Dallas.

"Whatever, let's go get our haircut!" stated Alex.

"Yeah-let's go!"

Chapter Twelve: The Atelier

Francine arrived at her parent's shop late the following morning, still high from her magical evening with Steven. "Hi Maman...hi Papa!" Francine shouted as she walked through the shop door and hung her jacket in the closet.

"We were wondering what time you were going to be here," Maman giggled.

"Oh, mon cheri...leave Francine alone," Papa said.

Francine then added, "I had a wonderful night last night at the restaurant and with Steven."

"It looks that way," Maman said, still giggling.

Francine ignored her Maman's teasing knowing full well that she was not being mean. After settling in, Francine started assembling the projects she intended to work on for the day. She also reached into her bag to retrieve the papers that Steven had given to her last night regarding the business agreement between Prentice-Hall and Francine Dubious. Francine reviewed the papers that were given to her, though a lot of it she really didn't understand.

Francine hands the papers to her papa, "Papa here are the papers that Mrs. Prentice-Hall's lawyer drew up regarding them helping me to open up my own atelier. Can you please take a look at them and see if everything looks good. I'm so happy to even have this opportunity, but let me know what you think, and if we should have someone else review it too?"

"First let me see what it says, just to make sure that we both understand what we're getting into," Papa interjected. "If necessary we can always have a lawyer look at it also."

Francine's papa unfolded the papers and took quite awhile reviewing them-periodically inserting sounds of acknowledgment as he proceeded.

"Well, Papa?" Francine asked anxious to hear his thoughts.

"I think that it's very fair. I also think that while yes, it is a business deal, they're really not looking for anything crazy. The amount of the loan will be returned from the monthly receipts after the bills have been paid. With them handling the books, it will allow yourself to be free to design and run the shop," Papa explained.

Francine's excitement far surpassed anything that needed to be ironed out in a contract. While Francine as her Papa discuss the specifics of this wonderful opportunity, she couldn't fight her mind from drifting back to certain moments from the previous night. It was like a constant loop of flashes from such a romantic night with Steven.

Papa had long since finished reviewing the contract, he asked Francine to sign it, and now the only thing left to do was hand-deliver them to Prentice-Hall's lawyers' office. Even as the papers were yet to be delivered, Francine had heard that the construction workers had begun working on the interiors of the shop; that's when it became real for her. This was happening.

Steven and Francine met several times now at the architect's office, once again reviewing the sketches that the interior designer created for the look for the new *atelier*. Francine was so excited, seeing the updated sketches with all of the corrections from the previous visit. "They're so beautiful." She stated holding the large boards in her hands. Francine taking her time to review every inch, seeing how her color choices were now coming alive, she really enjoyed seeing how the firm placed each specific color within her selected palette, from the walls to the carpets.

The trim would be a cream color, with splashes of Vogue Green (how perfect) and Cascade Green, with touches of pink. Everything from the signage to all of the packaging materials would carry her brand colors. She herself couldn't have dreamed of something so beautiful. It was clean, modern and a perfect reflection of Francine.

One of Francine's favorite areas was the main salon, with it's custom carpet which will be a sea of thick lush Cascade Green carpet with a band of Vogue Green around all of the edges. As clients enter the shop, they will be greeted with two cream colored curved sofas facing each other, so that the guests can easily review specific dresses on the models as they parade down the curved staircase.

After this particular meeting, that actually finished up early this time, Steven suggested they go by the job site to see how the actual construction process was going. Francine had been enjoying the whole process of creating her atelier, she feels very safe with Steven. Not only with his business knowledge, but also his general knowledge and support through this whole process.

Yes, it was his family money backing this venture. But Steven seems to be constantly referring to points within the project that would be better off for Francine in the long run. That meant so much to her, Steven watching out for Francine's best interest and not just what would save money. They both made their way out of the architect's office and proceeded to Steven's car, to head to the site.

As they neared the site, which was a separate dwelling on it's own on a main avenue in town. Steven was fortunate enough to find parking right in front. He jumped out, and ran around to the other side of the car to open the door for Francine.

As they both approached the double glass doors, Francine was immediately taken aback by a new sign that was already hanging on the front of the studio.

L'Atelier de Francine Dubois

Steven opened one of the glass doors for Francine, and as they both stepped in, Francine's breath was taken away in a sharp gasp. So much so that it was audible. Steven immediately turned to Francine and asked, "Are you okay?"

"Am I okay? Yes. I'm just shocked and speechless with how beautiful everything is. I know that we have seen sketches a million times, but to be here now, it's almost too much to handle." Francine raises her gloved hand to her mouth, and literally stepped back as though she is needing to sit.

Steven grabbed her arm to support her, "Are you sure you're fine? Let's just have you sit here for minute." He gently guided her over to a construction saw horse.

"Yes, I'm fine, but thanks for holding on to me. It really is more than I ever imagined it could be, it's so much larger too...that staircase...the wall of mirrors." Francine stopped talking abruptly when her voice cracked, on the verge of crying if she continued talking, and obviously she wanted to contain herself.

Though slightly uncomfortable, Steven completely understood. He changed the subject and escorted her around the studio. "Let's see what they have accomplished?" He took her arm, gently and very protectively guided her up the stairs. This is where the offices, changing areas for the models will be located, and of course the seamstresses will be positioned a little further back. Most of everything will be located up here. And the lower level will be the area to meet and greet clients, and of course private dressing rooms for guests. Along with the back room for the shipping and receiving, basically the dock area.

"Seamstresses? Offices? How many people are going to work here?" Francine asked.

Steven quickly replied, "Well you can't do this all by yourself, you will need a support staff. Your job is to design and make sure that the garments are made to your satisfaction."

"Yes...I completely understand, like I said I think I'm just over whelmed by all of this, I just hope that I don't disappoint anyone."

Steven bolstered her by saying, "Francine, your talent is the reason we're standing here today. My Aunt saw something in you and wanted to give you this opportunity. I know nothing about fashion but even I, can see that your talented and that you have a passion and a desire."

Francine didn't know what she liked more, the design of her new business or all of the time that she was spending with Steven. Francine especially loved it when the meetings ran late, because Steven always asked her if they could go and catch a quick bite to eat afterwards. This time with him was all so surreal. Her own business was being created in front of her eyes, with a man that was becoming more and more special as the days went on. Dare she admit that she might be falling love?

Chapter Thirteen: Presenting: L'Atelier de Francine DuBois

"Call for your Miss. Dubois." Peggy, Francine's assistant handed her the phone.

Francine had to take a second when she heard that. Though she was settling into this whole experience of being a creative director, designer, and business owner, she was not used to anybody referring to her as Miss Dubois.

Francine answered the call, "This is Francine?"

"Hi Francine, it's Steven are you getting excited about the opening?"

Oh Steven...there is so much to do still. I just don't know if we will be ready by Monday."

"Sure you will! Plus, whatever remains, will be finished up with time. Not every single detail needs to be in place and perfect for the doors to open."

"I hear that, I kind of understand. But, I really want it

to be perfect. I just want as much in place as possible... before everyone sees it, it will be their first impression and I want it to be a good one.

"Well, I was just there yesterday and to me all things feel that way, staff, models lined up, fabrics, all packaging materials. I know that there are some minor construction issues that have to be attended to, but like I said, it will all be worked out in time."

"You're the best Steven, I just think that I needed some reassurance, with the official opening next Monday and the added excitement and nervousness I have about this Friday's soft opening. I'm just a bit stressed."

"I understand, and you're doing a terrific job. Speaking of Friday, what time are we picking everyone up?" Steven asked.

"I would love that, or should I say, we would love that. I wanted to be here early, at least an hour before the guests start arriving. That is as long as I get all of the things done that I want to accomplish the day before." Francine explained.

"Sounds good," Steven replied. "Okay, we will arrive early on Friday to pick you and your parents up. Try to stay calm, all will be fine and work it's way out."

Peggy walked back into the room and announced, "Miss. Dubois, there is an issue down in shipping that needs your attention."

"Okay...got to go, I will talk to you later on honey," Francine stammered, now acutely aware of what she just said. As Francine hung the phone she thought, *Oh my... was that proper?*

The phrase haunted Francine as she proceeded down the main stairs to the salon. She scolded herself for being overly sensitive as she argued her own case in her head. *We have not kissed, but we spend a great deal of time together, and yes, it'd be nice for have him make the first romantic gesture, but he has...dinner, drinks, long glances.*

As Francine neared the bottom of the stairs, she was deluged by questions before she even hit the last stair. Her concerns of showing a romantic gesture towards Steven were replaced by the immediate business issues she had to tend to.

The big day is here, flowers are arriving in celebration of the soft opening that will occur that day. The shops' assistants busy placing everything for the big event, and they're literally running out of places to set the flowers. Everyone is busy with the finishing touches.

In the meantime, Francine's morning started out wanting to join her parents at the breakfast table. They were well into their second cup of coffee by the time she worked her way into the kitchen. The smell of coffee brewing and the sound of the eggs frying was so inviting to all of her senses. Maman looked radiant even though she was still in her robe and slippers. That radiance could possibly be from her excitement for Francine of what was all expected to occur on this magnificent day.

Francine poured herself a cup of freshly brewed coffee and sat with her Papa at the table. Papa reached out to grasp Francine's hand, connecting to her in a soft and gentle action that was so his style. Maman broke the stillness by asking Francine what her plans were for the day.

"I have an appointment this morning to have my hair and nails done." Francine continued, "After that I really just want to come home and take a bath and relax, until Steven comes by to pick us up."

The afternoon flew by, with time spent at the beauty shop, coming home bathing and relaxing and then preparing her dress for the big night. Francine wanted to make sure that she looked her best.

It was around 5:30 in the evening, when Francine heard the doorbell rang. Mr. Dubois opened the door to greet Steven and his Aunt Molly. He offered them both a drink, though they both declined. "S'il vous plait...please, sit, the ladies are still finishing up, but it shouldn't much longer."

As Papa instructed Steven and Aunt Molly in his thick French accent.

Steven and Aunt Molly made themselves comfortable in the living room as they took in the inviting and simple decor. The home, a classic small bungalow; built right after the war to provide more price efficient homes for the GI's when they returned home from Europe. The home was modestly decorated, and of course it reflected the style of the current times of the 1940's. Papa engaged them in small talk, then all of sudden Steven stopped talking and suddenly rose from the living room chair. Papa immediately noticed Steven's abrupt manner and turned to see what has captured his attention. They both went silent, as Francine descended the short staircase.

She was simply stunning, her gown of course-one of her own creations-a gorgeous aubergine satin strapless number with large side bow at her hip. Though the dress was mid-calf, it was the side bow that was attached to an over skirt that flowed elegantly over her body and onto the stair treads below. As she approached the living room and what felt like her awaiting audience, Francine finished off her look with long black gloves that ended just above her elbows, and her pearl earrings were the perfect finishing touch. Leaving her neck and decolletage free and unadorned-except for a hint of her haunting perfume.

Steven had never seen Francine look so incredibly beautiful before. Her raven hair was pinned up into a French twist, she looked regal and sophisticated; everything one expected from the presence of a highly sought after fashion designer.

A few minutes later her Maman made her debut, also looking so pretty. In fact, Papa's eyes were a-glow when he looked at her. After all of these years, she was still the prettiest girl in the room to him.

All of the ladies gathered together as Aunt Molly gushed over each other's gowns, but Steven needed to break-up the conversation because he realized that it was getting late and they needed to head over to the new shop.

The Dubois's, Aunt Molly, and Steven all drove together. For the Dubois's and Aunt Molly this would actually be their first time seeing everything pulled together and finished.

Steven pulled up to the storefront and jumped out, to appropriately let everybody out. Francine in the front seat first, then Aunt Molly in the back, followed by Francine's parents. Francine hired car valets, and even though they were an hour early their was someone there to hand off the keys too.

In fact one of the valets opened one of the shop's glass doors for Francine, to make her grand entrance. Though no guests had yet arrived yet, her staff broke out into applause at her arrival.

Francine blushes, and Steven instantly walked up from behind and slipped his arm around her waist to escort her in. Steven was so proud of her, and everything that she'd created. But most of all, he felt lucky enough to be the one by her side.

As Francine turned to see where everyone that she arrived with, had gone. She noticed instantly that Aunt Molly was literally non-stop talking and gasping over every detail, as she pointed out everything from signage, to the carpet, to the ladies of the shop. Then Francine turned to locate her Maman and Papa, who she found standing by the front door still, with tears streaming down their faces.

Francine dropped everything to go to them, and immediately started speaking to them in French. She asked them if they were okay. They were both were so overcome with emotion that they were literally speechless for several moments.

"It's magnificent Francine, we're so proud," Papa said. "We could have never dreamed this for you."

Maman, turned her back because she was unable to hold back her emotions. Francine hugged her, knowing how full of pride she was of Francine in this moment. After a minute or two, Maman finally collected herself and continued into the showroom.

Francine was soon pulled into multiple areas to tend to one thing after another. Maman and Papa, walked up to every single element in the room, careful not to miss a thing. It was as though they were in their own private bubble, completely immune to what was occurring all around them. The staff and servers all scurried about tending to their necessary duties, and aiding in all areas making sure that the evening would be a success. Aunt Molly had now exhausted herself and decided to sit. The doors were now open and soon the reality of the that moment would occur, if not that evening...most definitely the next day.

Chapter Fourteen: Designed to Fit... Loved for the Style!

The salon had been open for a week now. Francine arrived early everyday, always to be greeted by her secretary Peggy, as soon as she pushed open her office door.

Peggy immediately handed Francine about 20 messages and numerous cards, "Those are the ones that arrived since yesterday right after you left."

The adoration and well wishes had been so endearing. Francine was still glowing and thrilled by the response to her Atelier. The seamstresses were already hard at work with all of the fitting appointments that were scheduled. Mrs. Prentice-Hall, was not only a client, but of course a backer, which has served as a built in self-promoting marketing machine. If this was any indication of what is to come, there was no telling where it would go. Because there is no fashion, without people.

Francine was sketching out some new design concepts

when Peggy interrupted her over the intercom, informing her that Steven was on the phone. Francine picked up the line, "Now how did you know that I wanted to hear the sound of your voice?"

"Well, then maybe you need to see me too. How about lunch somewhere just us?" Steven asked.

"Absolutely," Francine replied. "When will you be by to pick me up?"

"How about 30 minutes?"

"Perfect, see you in a few!"

Francine loved this feeling, of truly connecting to Steven more and more each day! Hoping, now that the studio was open, maybe she would now start to see Steven on a more romantic standpoint. Only time will tell! Francine finishes up her sketches and ran into the powder room to check her make-up, before her lunch date with Steven.

Just as she finished up rouging her lips, Steven's voice echoed up to her as he greeted the staff in the main part of the studio. Francine proceeded down the stairs to meet him. They both caught each other's eye, and exchanged hellos. When Steven leaned in to kiss Francine's lips, she was startled, but quite happy. Once they were outside, Steven opened the car door for Francine, she loved the fact that he continued to put her comfort first and making her feel special. As they pulled away from the curb, he asked her what she was in the mood for, for lunch.

"You haven't disappointed me so far, surprise me," Francine stated with a seductive grin.

"Oh...I would love too, and plus I really enjoy sharing new experiences with you."

They pulled into the restaurant parking lot and Steven once again, quickly ran around to the other side of the car to open Francine's door. Francine thought that Steven was definitely being engaging and directing this particular encounter in more of a romantic tone, then other times. Not that he'd ever been anything less than a gentleman, but his personal touches seemed different this time.

Steven was definitely being engaging and directing this particular encounter in more of romantic tone, than previous other times. Not that he'd ever been anything less than a gentleman, but his personal touches seem different now.

As they both entered the restaurant, Francine was immediately impressed with the décor and the overall environment of this particular place. Her favorite touch were the lamps located in the center of the tables, instead of bright overhead lighting. They were both escorted to a secluded booth and were handed menus. They exchange small talk as they both reviewed the menu.

"So, is there anything that you would recommend?" Francine asked playfully.

"Absolutely." Steven replied. "The seafood here is spectacular, and if you just want something light...then the perhaps the shrimp salad."

"Sounds perfect."

The waiter approached the table, Steven gave him their order as he simultaneously handed back the menus. The room was rich with smoke as it danced in the air, that was highlighted by the subtle light coming from the lamps on the tables. The air was also thick with the energy of "forgetting." Forgetting about time, life's partners, and problems.

Francine breaks the silence, "This place is somewhere one could get lost in, it's dark and mysterious and dare I say a touch romantic."

"I'm glad that you find it romantic," Steven said, "because that's one of the reasons I wanted to see you today."

Francine is filled with anticipation in what Steven will say next. Will her intuition be correct? Are they both on the same page? She leans forward, places her elbows on the table, and tilts her head. She doesn't want to miss a word.

"Really?" Francine replied.

Steven smiled, "Yes, I just wanted to let you know that

I have enjoyed spending these last weeks with you as we created your business. I found myself missing not seeing you everyday and spending time together for dinner."

"Me too," as Francine smiled and leaned in even more towards Steven, anxious to hear what he will say next. She noticed that a small bead of sweat began to run down the side of his face.

"I like you very much," Steven continued, "and I feel that there is a mutual connection here."

"Yes," Francine agreed.

"Well, I would like to take our connection to the next level, plus, I would like us to be exclusive." Steven states to Francine as he takes another sip of liquid courage. His hand shakes just a touch as the ice hits the side of the glass.

Francine nodded and took his hand, "I would like the same thing, I too feel a strong connection between us. I would love it if we could continue to see each privately and date."

"I'm so glad." Steven replied, "I wanted to tell you the night of your opening. I knew then, that I wanted you all to myself. But, that wasn't the best time, but here we are, and I'm so glad and relieved that we're moving forward together."

"Me too."

Chapter Fifteen:
One Special Night!

francine and Steven had been seeing each other now exclusively for several months. But, on this one particular "date" that they both spent exploring Chicago together, did not end up being just like any other "date."

It began with them playing who has a better cab, with the numerous amount of times they'd got in and out of those large checker and yellow cabs. While visiting the Field Museum, the Art Institute and having lunch on Michigan Avenue, they enjoyed the energy of the city. The hustle of people rushing to business appointments, lunch dates and shopping. The air thick with humidity and exhaust as the summer's heat was already soaring for the day. But nothing can ruin Francine's joy of spending the day with a man that she was madly in love with.

It was now dusk, Francine's favorite time of day. A car approached them, with a private driver to take them out to a place called Ravinia. Steven explained to her that it was a music park about 30 minutes North of Chicago.

Little did she know that Steven had an "evening" picnic all prepared for them both after they arrived. He also hired someone to set up a table, and serve them. This was going to be one of the most elegant picnics Francine will ever be on.

As the car pulled up to the front gate of the park, their driver dropped them off. It was a beautiful summer evening as the stars blanketed the sky, providing the most romantic backdrop. Ravinia, with live music and picnicking, was not your ordinary type of music park. Those who went to Ravinia, could either select seats under the mezzanine, or in the lawn area. The lawn section was a favorite for those who like to bring their own table, chairs, food and some even had candelabras for a total one-of-a-kind experience.

Steven also arranged to have candlelight and flowers already placed on the table. There was no detail that'd escaped Steven's imagination for that evening; he wanted everything just so. The Chicago Symphony Orchestra played compilations from Schubert and Bach-which happened to be some of Francine's favorite classical pieces. They were finishing up their "picnic," when a particular song started to play that got Francine's attention right away. Steven noticed this, so he took it as his clue to pull his chair next to hers. They sat in silence listening to the beauty of the string section as the violin concerto was played.

Steven tightened his hug on Francine as he took in the beauty of the night, and Francine.

It was intoxicating for her also, the smell of his cologne, the night stars, the music. She was thinking how could today get any better than this-when Steven whispered in her ear, "Will you marry me?"

Francine pulled back and gasped. With that gasp, her eyes filled with tears. She is awestruck. Awestruck, she somehow managed to say the words "YES! Oh my...yes... with all of my heart."

Francine wrapped her arms around Steven's neck, practically choking him. They both hugged as Francine continued to weep.

"I hope those are happy tears," Steven said, smiling.

Francine nodded, too overcome with joy to speak. They just continued to embrace each other, both knowing now they are now truly connected forever.

Steven reached into his pocket to retrieve a small box and opened it to show Francine, who clutched her hands under her chin in anticipation-while blinking away tears. He placed the beautiful yellow gold setting with large center diamond, flanked by smaller diamonds on the side-on her finger.

Awed by it's beauty, Francine couldn't stop looking at

her hand. She continuously waved her left hand in the air, while she tried to figure out which was more shiny, her new ring or the moonlight; the rays seemed dim by comparison. Those sitting in close proximity to them on lawn, congratulate both Francine and Steven. Of course, Steven extended a gracious thank to them all, as Francine continued to admire her hand.

Steven once again pulled Francine in tight, holding her as though he was afraid that the love that was radiating from them will somehow seep out. The orchestra continued to play, the violins in particular were a strong, seductive presence in the background that lulled them all into an extended state of euphoria.

Once the concert ended, Steven called over the gentleman that arranged all preparations, requesting that he please pack everything up. Steven then reached into his pocket and released the clip that held his money together and gave him an ample amount. Steven then guided Francine back to the park entry gates. They found his car, that he had planned ahead of time to leave by the front of the park. Steven hadn't missed a step on this incredible adventure.

He opened the passenger's side door to let Francine in, when suddenly he swept her tightly in his arms. He knew that he was safe from peering eyes, comfortable enough to embrace her. He literally engulfed her with his physical presence, pressing her hard against the car, and kissing her with such intensity that soft moans of pain and pleasure came from Francine.

Steven stopped, pulled back a few inches from Francine and looked deeply into her eyes, "I couldn't wait any longer to do that. The ring that I gave you symbolizes my desire for our future together with you, and I don't want this evening to end."

"Neither do I," Francine replied.

Steven opened the car and placed Francine gently in the passenger seat, then he quickly ran around his car to get into the driver's seat. Before they pulled away Steven took a moment to release car's top. Francine rested her head on his shoulder as they pulled away. Everything was right with the world. The warm night air blowing through their hair, the stars, the music and of course the engagement. They drove away in silence, with an incredible peaceful knowing that tonight would be one of the greatest nights they will experience together.

Chapter Sixteen: Bonfire at Wilmette Beach

Dallas and Alex were burning away the hours hanging out in "the hideaway," doing nothing but mindless online searching, when a text arrived from Zach. Dallas sat up immediately, excited and a slight bit nervous as she announced each individual text:

Do you want to go to a bonfire Thursday night?

Sure! Dallas replied.

Great pick u up at 8!

Sounds good!

Dallas immediately starts pounding the floor with her feet and screams, "NICE!"

"I'm so glad that we're actually going to hang out before the dance. That way we can get any of that first encounter weird awkwardness between us, out of the way then."

"Totally agree," Alex replied.

With that, the girls went into full blown what I'm I going to wear...mode! Dallas immediately jumped up, and started ripping through her make-shift closet which was an old armoire that'd been sitting empty collecting dust in the corner.

"If we can't find something here, I can go downstairs to my room and see what's still hanging in my closet. I usually keep me favorite things up here," Dallas said.

Soon clothes going flying. Alex sitting on the divan, watched the "air" show as one item after another took flight from the disapproval of Dallas.

"This is perfect," shouts Dallas.

"Cool, go try it on and let's see what it looks like."

Dallas ran behind the folding screen, proceeded to throw her jeans over the edge of the screen. After a few minutes she appeared from behind in a super cute outfit; a white thick oversized cotton turtleneck, with a medium toned pink skinny jean.

"Well...what do you think?" Dallas asked.

"That's perfect," Alex said, "it looks great against your dark hair."

With a pair of flips...this "fit" is "on point."

"Agreed...LOVE!"

Dallas went back behind the screen and changed back into the clothes that she'd had on before the much needed pop-up fashion show. She came back around the screen and they went back into their usual positions, to resume hammering away on their laptops.

"Holy crap," Dallas suddenly shrieked, "some troll is posting nasty comments about me on social."

"Shut up, seriously?" Alex took the phone from Dallas and reads the screen.

"OMG...they're talking about the dance. Girl, they're just jealous because your going with Zach."

"Yeah your right," Dallas agreed "but it's hard to ignore what they're saying."

"True, just find something else to look at."

Dallas found something else to occupy her time with and soon those negative comments fell to the past.

Thursday came faster than Dallas expected. She woke early that morning excited about her date that would happen later on with Zach, and feeling extra confident after already having done the 'date outfit' precheck.

Dallas left for school and even though there were moments during the day where time dragged, the day really did go by quite fast. When the last bell rang, Dallas grabbed her backpack and hurried for the parking lot. Just as she got into her Jeep, her phone chimed that a text had arrived from Alex. Dallas opened it:

Enjoy the date...can't wait to hear all about it!

As Dallas backed out of the parking lot she sent Alex a thumbs up emoji, but her mind was on what will be happening later on, day dreaming as she drove, about what the night might bring. After pulling into the her driveway at home, Dallas jumped out of the car, and headed for the front door, and pushed it open.

"Hello!" she shouted, but she didn't wait to see if anyone was there to respond.

She ran, up the stairs to her bohemian hideaway, finished up her after school routine, then checked her phone for any possible incoming texts from Zach – nothing yet. Dallas then threw herself on the divan to stare out the huge window. That particular window spanned into an eight foot half-circle located in the center of her hideaway. This was her all-time favorite look-out point. Because her house was the tallest in the neighborhood she could see miles of the magnificent lakefront. Dallas could, and had, spent hours just laying up there staring out the window.

The sun was now positioned in the front of the house, making it possible to see endless miles of lakefront. As Dallas laid there staring out the window, her body grew heavy and she soon drifted off to sleep.

The headlights were now reflecting rocks and sand, as the sound of breaking waves against the shore grew louder. Dallas looked over at Zach as he put the car in park, and her first thought was about how beautiful the reflection of the dash lights were on his face, it was hypnotic to her. Who was this man? And why did he have such a hold on her heart?

Zach reached over and turned on the radio, which broke the silence. But not in a bad way, it added another layer of tranquility to an already blissful evening.

There was a peace she felt in his presence, nothing forced, rushed, or even trite about them being together. Zach was very comfortable with who he was. He had a way of making those around him also feel comfortable. Dallas, really wasn't listening for any specific words within the songs playing on the radio...it was just the melody that soothed her and added to their experience.

Zach reached over and took her hand, and they just sat there enjoying their time together, just being!

There was a hard knock at the door...Dallas...Dallas! Dallas's mom jolted her from her dream.

"Dallas...are you awake....it's 6:30."

While her Mom continued knocking, Dallas stirred and mumbled, "Yes!" Still very much half-asleep and kind of upset that she was so abruptly woken from her nap.

Mainly because she was really enjoying that dream.

"Oh gosh...I should get up..." she suddenly realized. "WHAT TIME DID YOU SAY IT WAS, Mom?"

"6:30!"

Dallas bolted into a sitting position to confirm the time on her phone, as well as check for any last minute texts from Zach. "Cool...still plenty of time to get ready."

Dallas kicked into a higher gear and worked her way downstairs to get ready in her bedroom, even though she preferred "the hideaway." She rushed through the halls and pushed open her bedroom door; a space that at times seemed foreign to her because she spent so much time in "the hideaway." She quickly turned on a couple of lights to see. She then took a moment and sat on the edge of her bed, collecting her thoughts. She glanced around the room taking in every detail. Remembering how her mom recreated her room as a surprise when she went away to camp in the summer. Dallas realized that she needed to get going so she started the water for the shower and stepped in, now becoming invigorated and excited about the date, as the water hit her.

At 8 o'clock sharp, the doorbell rang. Barely hearing the bell from her bedroom, Dallas knew she needed to step it up. She was dressed, her hair dried and styled, and was just finishing up her make-up when her mom screams up the stairs that Zach was here. Dallas tried to acknowledge her mom but doubted that she'd heard her.

Dallas's mom answers the door and introduces herself, "Hi Zach nice to meet you, I'm Dallas's mom. "Zach...go ahead and have a seat anywhere you like in the living room," her Mom told him, "I'm sure that Dallas will be down soon."

Zach found a chair and threw himself into it, and immediately pulled out his phone and started to scroll through it.

Dallas's mom read that as a signal to leave him alone, she wouldn't have any of that.

"So, Zach," she said, "what time will you be bringing Dallas home and where are you two both headed out to?"

Zach knows that he needed to pay attention, so he put his phone down and promptly answered her. "Would twelve be okay?"

"Let's make it 11:30...it's a school night."

Zach nodded. "Yes, I totally understand."

"And where are you both heading off to?"

"A bonfire at Wilmette beach."

As Zach answered, Dallas came bouncing down the stairs. His attention was then immediately drawn to the stairs, and how pretty Dallas looked.

"Mom, please stop grilling Zach."

Her mom stopped doing whatever fake busy-work she was doing to occupy her time and reason to stay in the room. Turns to Dallas with her hand on her hip, "Dallas...I'm not grilling him, I'm simply doing my Mom job!"

Dallas lifted an eyebrow, "Well...did you get the answers that you needed?"

"Yes," her Mom replied. "Please be careful, and Dallas I will see you at 11:30."

"11:30?"

"Yep...sharp! And no drinking!"

"Bye, Mom."

"Bye," Zach called back, "it was nice meeting you."

"Bye, have fun guys."

Dallas and Zach made their way out the door and to the car. Zach reached in to open the car door for Dallas. As she jumped in, buckled her seat belt she was very impressed with the fact that his car was so clean.

After Zach hopped into the driver's seat and pulled away, it all began to feel a little "deja vu-ish," perhaps because she'd just had a dream very similar to this experience about a couple of hours ago. She glanced towards Zach, admiring the fact that his facial features were lit up by the dash board lights. OMG...this is so weird, and comfortable in an odd way.

Within minutes they arrive at Wilmette Beach. The

sound of the water crashing against the shore and the laughter coming from the darkness guided them. They both walked down a long ramp to the beach front, Dallas noticed that the breeze was a lot colder coming off of the lake. She was very happy to be wearing a heavier sweater at this point. Even the sand felt cold, as Dallas took her sandals off...now regretting that choice. They headed towards the bonfire, where about thirty people were standing around the fire pit. Zach proudly took Dallas' hand and guided her towards the group he was meeting up with, and introduced everyone to Dallas one by one.

The night flew by. After saying their good-byes, Zach and Dallas made their way back up the concrete ramp to the parking lot.

Once again he was a perfect gentleman, opening car doors, never being too aggressive. Dallas couldn't help to think how lucky she was to be able to meet such a great guy, as she waited for him to get into the driver's seat, no wonder the trolls on the social media are so jealous. She was so glad that the night had gone smooth and that their energy really meshed. This way when they attend the dance, there wouldn't be any awkward first stages of getting to know one another.

Then again...that didn't even happen tonight. It worked out just fine...with no effort.

Chapter Seventeen: We're Engaged!

"Oh good the lights are still on," Francine said as she and Steven burst through the front door. "We're engaged!"

Her declaration landed on an empty living room; apparently they had already gone to bed. Francine hurried to her parent's room and dragged them out to the living room all blurry-eyed, to see her ring.

Rubbing their eye's, confused by the disruption, it took a few moments for her parents to connect the major news their daughter was trying to share. Then outburst of happiness filled the room. In fact, Maman had completely forgotten that she was not really presentable to see Steven with her hair filled with pin curls. Though as soon as she saw the ring, she started crying in excitement for her daughter's future.

"Oh Maman, please don't cry," Francine implored her.

"But this is what I'm supposed to do...*tres magnifique!*"

Maman and Papa start talking to each other in French

and of course Francine joined in.

Steven can hardly grasp what is being said in the tidal wave of *c'est bon's*, flying about.

Francine cried with her Maman, Papa walked over to hug Steven while the ladies fell to the sofa in a puddle of tears.

"Steven, you made Francine and of course us, very happy."

"No," Steven said, "she has made me very happy."

Maman got up to hug Steven, "Merci, thank you, Francine is so happy, I'm so happy." Maman cried even harder.

Papa broke up the crying by saying, "Let's have a toast, Champagne!"

"I'll get the glasses," shouted Maman.

Francine looked to Steven, almost apologetic. Steven understood completely, as Francine was their only daughter this would be a once in a lifetime situation for them.

Papa returned from the kitchen carrying the bottle of Champagne, Maman followed with four glasses that clanked together all the way back into the living room. Papa pops the cork and everyone cheered! Papa takes one of the glasses from Maman and begins to pour and pass around the glasses. Once everyone has a glass, a momentous and simultaneous "cheers," rings out!

Steven was the first to finish and as he put his glass down, he then proceeded to excuse himself from the celebration.

"Oh *oui*, yes, yes, yes!" Maman and Papa say in unison.

Steven took Francine's hand and guided her to the door. As they, looked deeply into each others eye's. Steven kissed Francine on the lips then pulled back to say, "Thank you for making this the best night of my life."

Francine stood in the threshold of her parent's home, talking with Steven. Tears filled her eyes and though the words feel weak in comparison to the emotions within her, she manages eek out, "No thank you...for this magical night." She lifted his hand to her cheek and kissed the inside of his palm.

Steven pulled away reluctantly, smiled, then worked his way back to his car. As he opened his car door, he stopped short of getting in, paused and turned to look back at Francine, full of happiness and pride that Francine would now be his bride.

The next morning Francine and the entire Dubois family were still a glow from the exciting news. Maman was busy in the kitchen making and coffee, while Papa was reading the paper.

Maman breaks the morning quiet when Francine entered the kitchen, "Are you going into your shop today?"

"Oh yes, I need to start designing my wedding dress," Francine replied. "Not like I haven't been doing it a million times in my head, but now I actually need to get something draped out in muslin."

"Oui, c'est bon," Maman stated with a full smile, as she continued finishing up Papa's breakfast and placed it on the table in front of him. "Francine, *voulex-vous des oeufs?"*

"Non, merci." Francine replied.

"Okay, I'm off to the *atelier,* see you both after work." Francine shouted, *"Au revoir...au revoir."*

Francine grabbed her bag and some sketches that she had been working on, and ran out the door. As she jumped into the car, she reminded herself to take a moment and to stay present. She understood that this time will go by fast and as soon as she completed that thought, the sound of a blaring car horn jolted her back into reality. The reality was that she'd just run a red light. Francine adjusted herself in the seat, and instantly realized that she needed to concentrate on the road not on her wedding dress and all that was to come.

As the owner of the *atelier,* Francine could park anywhere she would like, while the employees had to park in the back. This always felt awkward and out of character for Francine, who'd came from such a practical and humble background. She felt that their was no need to set herself apart from others, nor evoke any kind entitlement.

So, as Francine pulled open the back door, she was instantly inundated with "hello's" and questions. She worked her way up the main salon stairs and to her office. Francine threw her sketches on her drawing table, then took off her gloves one finger at a time, and removed her hat too. When not seeing clients, she liked to wear a white smock over her clothes, to protect her outfit, as well as to connect to her associates. All seamstresses in the atelier wore them, to protect the garments. It was mainly for preventing dye cast-off from their own clothes.

Francine pulled the sketches out of her portfolio and placed them on the drafting table. A few moments later, Peggy her secretary, walked in to hand her all of her new phone messages and to discuss any new and pertinent information regarding clients, fabrics, and any employee issues for that day.

"Peggy, can you help me with a couple of ideas I have for a wedding gown?"

"I didn't know that you were adding a wedding dress to the next season's line?"

"Actually it's mine." Francine flashed a broad smile, "Steven proposed last night."

"Oh my gosh…seriously…let me see the ring…it's so beautiful," Peggy shrieked. "Yes, yes let me see the sketches. Then I need to hear all of the details."

Francine showed Peggy one by one everything that she had sketched. Francine had these sketches at home for a while, keeping them from the public like silent wishes. But now that she was a officially engaged, they could be discussed openly.

Peggy studied each sketch carefully as Francine watched Peggy's face for any tell-tale signs that might denote one is better than the other. She squinted with desperation in search of direction from Peggy.

Peggy placed the drawings down, takes off her glasses and said, "They're all fantastic, they each have there own unique aspect…that truly makes them special."

"That's not helping me, Peggy," Francine said.

"I understand."

Peggy held up two of her favorites, which both happen to be in lace with long sheer sleeves. "If you were to force me to choose…I would choose this one and this one."

"Well, that's a start," Francine nodded. "Okay send up Jocelyn the head seamstress so that I can get her started working on a muslin draping."

"Absolutely," Peggy said. "So excited for you both, congratulations."

"Thanks, Peggy...I'm so excited too."

Within minutes Jocelyn was in Francine's office with sketchbook and measuring tape in hand, tools that go with her everywhere.

"Hi Jocelyn, I have some new sketches I would like you to see."

Jocelyn took a minute and studied the sketches that were now strewn across the floor. She removed her glasses and reviewed them. These are fabulous are you adding a wedding dress to the line?"

"No," Francine said, "this is a custom piece...for me!"

"Oh, Miss. Dubois, this is so fabulous I'm so happy for you, congratulations."

"Thank you, Jocelyn. What I would like you to do is create a muslin draping of both of these. I will make my decision based on the two designs...we might even combine some of both of their elements into one."

"Right away Miss Dubois."

Jocelyn worked her way back to the production area and like a giddy school girl proceeded to tell the other seamstresses the good news.

"Ladies, even though this is exciting news, we all need to be respectful of the fact that she has not yet shared her engagement news publicly. So, we need not discuss this with others. Do you understand?"

"Yes...yes...yes...yes," as all of the fellow seamstress sound off.

"Now with that said we have some sketches from Miss Dubois that we all need to review. We're going to need to drape both of these out. So, Sophia I will be assigning you this dress, and Elizabeth you will have this one," as Jocelyn handed them their individual designs.

Francine walked through the doorway, all of the ladies start to clap, "Thank you, that's very sweet. I look forward to reviewing the garments, but I also want it to be known that all client garments must take precedent."

"We're all very happy for you," Jocelyn continued, "And these dresses will be made with great love."

All of the ladies started to clap again.

Francine blushed and nodded as she left to head back to her office.

Chapter Eighteen: On the Corner of Cozy and Got to Have it!

The engagement announcement made the New York Times newspaper. Between wedding plans and the new spring line, Francine was being pulled thin. In fact, some days Francine didn't even have time for lunch. By the time she arrived home at night, she barely had enough energy to drag herself into a much needed bubble bath.

Francine was just leaving the workroom after reviewing the muslin samples of her final two choices for her wedding gown, when Peggy stopped her.

"Steven is on the phone for you."

"Great I will get it in my office." Francine walked towards her office and closed the door. Francine plopped herself down behind her desk in her custom swivel desk chair. A beautiful office designed for a beautiful lady, in its delicate shades of pinks and greens. Her desk a large mahogany writing desk with a large center drawer for all the appropriate office supplies, and personalized station-ary. Francine picked up the phone and removed her ear-ring while adding just a touch of sultriness to her voice. "Hello, my darling are you already missing the sound of my voice?"

"Yes," Steven replied, "how did you know?"

"By how early you're calling."

"Well, there is a reason, besides the desire to hear your voice."

"Do tell!"

"I know that this is sudden, but I found something that I would like you to see."

Francine cocked her head. "Okay, do I get any hints?"

"One," Steven said, "because I want this to be a surprise."

"Okay, is it bigger than a bread box?"

"Oh my gosh yes! In fact you can fit a ton of bread box-es in it."

"Oh really, now you definitely have my interest peaked."

"Great I will be there to pick you up around 2:00. How does that sound?"

"Sounds good, my love, see you then."

Francine hung up the phone and leaned back in her chair. Enjoying the quiet, almost as much as just having talked to Steven. Her office is a secluded sanctuary for the times when she needs to close off the noise and constant chatter, that is fashion.

No phone constantly ringing, no one asking her questions, nor any needy customers on the floor insisting on getting Francine's personal attention.

Reality crashes in on her bliss moments later with the sound of a buzzer from Peggy's desk.

"Francine? Your needed in alterations."

With that abrupt interruption, Francine collected herself and headed down to the first floor salon's dressing rooms. She checked her hair and lipstick in the mirror before she walked downstairs. As she exited, she told Peggy, "Thank you, and I will be leaving when Steven gets here around 2:00. I do not know if I will be back."

"Okay, I understand," Peggy replied.

Francine worked her way downstairs to the main dressing rooms to see what the client needed. Francine knocked on DR 4, one of the largest rooms. As she entered the dressing room, she noticed one of her seamstresses trying to zip or unzip the client's skirt. But after looking it became clear that the client had caught her diamond bracelet in the metal tracks of the zipper.

"Oh my, what do we have here?" Francine asked.

"Miss. Dubois, I'm so glad that you here, it seems that this skirt that you created has ruined my bracelet."

Francine liftd an eyebrow. "Really? The skirt ruined your bracelet? Now how did that happen?"

"I don't know, if I did I wouldn't be in this position to begin with. You must simply get me out of this horrible situation."

"Yes, of course," Francine said, "it would be a little difficult to get home that way too."

The customer shot Francine a disapproving look, but Francine continued to see if there was anything more that she could do.

Francine knew that the client was in good hands with one of her best seamstresses. Seeing that the client was growing rapidly impatient and embarrassed, however, Francine instructed the seamstress to cut her out of the skirt.

"Once the skirt is removed, the seamstress will be able to dislodge the bracelet better," Francine explained.

"I sure hope so, the woman said, "this has been very frustrating."

Francine nodded. "I understand completely, please come back another time, and I will make sure that you are given a very nice discount for all of your inconvenience."

"I certainly hope so." As the client swiftly turned up her face in her best false bravado presentation.

Francine has had experience dealing with difficult clients before, especially those that were high maintenance on top of it. Most of their demands came from an impatient disposition, demanding a certain level of service for the dollars they spend. Which unfortunately was accompanied by a great deal of entitlement with very little flexibility.

Francine had a great ability to stay flexible in the land of, "I want it, the way I want it." Well-aware that many were firm in their own way of thinking and not always aligned nor sensitive to those around them.

The salon's chimes rang out, signaling where Francine needed to be. She headed to the center of the salon where she was instantly greeted with a large bouquet of white roses.

"Oh my, those are so beautiful!" Francine said.

She soon discovered that Steven was the one responsible for purchasing them, and delivering them too. Not trusting that a delivery person would be able to get them there in time.

"Steven, I can barely see you, they're magnificent."

"I'm glad," Steven replied, "but their beauty pales in your presence."

"Oh Steven, you're beyond sweet and charming."

"Please call Peggy down here to place these in my office

behind my desk, thank you," Francine directed one of the salon consultants. "Oh, and can you have her bring down my purse and gloves?"

Steven placed his hand against the small of Francine's back and guided her off to a more private area of the salon to talk to her. "So, besides the desire to see you, I want to show you something so are you ready to step away for a little while?"

"Sure, but what's with all the mystery? Francine asked. "Where are we going?"

"Well, I'd rather show you. I won't be able to do it justice by trying to explain."

"Okay, then let's go." As Francine said that, one of the consultants handed Francine her gloves and purse and soon they were both headed out the door – but off to where?

"Maybe I should blind fold you?" Steven said after helping Francine into the car and running to the driver's side to get in.

"No," Francine protested, smiling. "I'm curious and excited let's just go."

"Okay!"

Steven puts the car's top down, and Francine with out missing a beat, pulls a scarf and sunglasses from her purse. She tilted the rear view mirror in her direction to check to see if she positioned her scarf correctly.

Steven immediately barked, "Hey, I need that!"

"Just a second."

Steven had chosen a great day weather – wise. In fact, the company and the scenery were all just perfect. Steven makes his way down major streets, drives and lanes, turning and then turning again, really confusing Francine. Finally he pulls over on this magnificent tree lined street filled with large homes on even larger pieces of land.

"Well, we're almost there. Can I get you to at least close your eyes?"

"Oh Steven, you're so silly. Okay, fine, but no blind fold." With that Francine closed her eye's"

"Now, no peeking." Steven pulled away from the curb as the giant oaks and maples created a spectacular canopy to drive under, then the car slowed again.

"Can I open my eyes yet?" Francine asked.

"In two minutes." The car then gently turned left into what must have been a driveway. Steven then says, "Okay you can open your eyes now."

Francine opens her eyes and gasps, rising off her seat as though the grandeur of the home was summoning her forth. Almost completely standing now, supported herself by holding the frame of the windshield.

Steven noticed the look on her face and immediately knows that he was correct in his decision; this was something that she needed to see.

Francine remained speechless as she took in every inch of the home, until Steven broke the silence by asking her:

"Do you want to go in and see it?"

"Oh my yes."

Steven pulled the car through the *porte-cochere*.

Francine could hardly wait until the car came to a complete stop, in order for her to get out.

Steven placed the car in park and jumped out himself. They both walked up to the door on the side of the home, Francine was completely captivated by the home. The richness of the dark brick in it's many hues of brown, the climbing ivy that went on forever, and especially the huge limbering trees. Everything was magnificent. Steven reached for the doorknob as they proceed to walk into the home.

Francine was the first to enter, slowly dragging a hand along the walls while scanning every room, as they both ventured through together. Francine remained quiet, concentrating on what the home had to offer. By the time they'd completed the first floor, Steven turned to Francine and stated, "Well? What do you think? I hope you like it."

"I do," Francine replied.

"Good, it's yours!"

Francine froze, and abruptly turned her head toward Steven, "What? This is our home?"

"Yes. As soon as I saw it I knew that you would love it. I fell in love with it the first time I saw it, just like when I first saw you."

"Oh Steven, this is amazing." Francine leaped into his arms and they kissed, long, hard and passionate.

"Come, you need to see my favorite part of this house." Steven grabbed Francine's hand and together they took the stairs upwards; first fight, second flight, then finally the third. They wound around a hallway until Steven finally stopped. They both stopped at a door at the what felt like was the very end of the house. It was a very simple door, it almost felt out of place for the rest of the house. Steven reaches down slowly grasping the door handle,opening what felt like a secret room.

The door opened and instantly light poured through the break in the door, causing them both to recoil back. Their eye's needed to adjust to extreme brightness. Francine entered first, Steven followed closely behind her.

"This is spectacular," Francine said, "The view is amazing, this room is so incredible, this whole house is. Steven you have found us such a beautiful home. And my favorite part is that it needs a little TLC. We can create it the way we want it to look."

Steven smiled, "I'm so glad that you like it, and yes, this top floor really needs some major love. But like you said we can make it ours before we move in."

"Steven, it's more than I could have ever imagined."

"Another thing too," Steven continued, "there is a guest house out back and if you would like your parents to be close, we can offer them that space."

Francine started to cry, "Steven you have made all my dreams come true, even dreams that I never even thought possible, because they would have seemed so far out of reach for me."

Steven walked over and embraced Francine, "No Francine you have made all of my dreams come true. I never thought I could love like this. You brought such happiness to my life, and in some small way this is my way of thanking you. I love you very much, and I'm so happy that we will spend our life together."

"Me too, Steven."

Francine and Steven embraced each other, their hearts and breath, in sync, connected as one, for all of time. Francine pulled out of the embrace as they both took in the view of Lake Michigan, Steven now searching in his pocket for his handkerchief to remove the lipstick from his mouth.

"I think that we need to make this unique space into some kind of secret room, a hide-a-way, just for us. A place we can both escape too. A place where we can lock away the rest of the world and just be together watching the water."

"Sounds like heaven," Steven said, "let's do it."

Chapter Nineteen: Now, Let's Get the Wedding Plans On!

F rancine quickly checked her watch, then told the other seamstresses that they're all right on track, and that she would review and sign off on the final elements for her wedding dress tomorrow. With that she stated her good-bye's and she ran to her office to grab her purse and she was off, to meet Steven and his Aunt for dinner.

As Francine pulled through the powerful iron gates of the Prentice-Hall estate, shocked at how fast she had gotten there without even paying attention. It was as though she was on auto-pilot. She pulled up the driveway and parked, she knew that she needed to take a minute, take a breath to reconnect to the moment, and at how much has changed in such a short period of time. Just a few months ago, she'd taken a street car here and bashfully worked her way up the front steps to this beautiful large mansion.

After taking a couple of quiet moments in the car, melting into the driver's seat, she realized she needed to get in the house for the dinner gathering. Francine worked her way back up those stairs that so intimated her such a short time ago. This time, she'd climbed them in a completely different manner. As a soon to be member of this prestigious family.

Francine, centered herself with a deep breath and proceeded to ring the bell. Within, moments one of the servants answered the door and greeted her by name.

"Welcome, Miss. Dubois, everyone is in the main salon, waiting for you."

Francine nodded when the servant stepped aside to let her pass. "Thank you, so very much."

As Francine passed through the grand marble floor entry and they both headed in the direction of the formal living room area. Steven was the first to see her and instantly stopped talking to his Aunt and stood up. He approached her, "Hello beautiful. How is my soon to be wife today?"

"Hello, my love," Francine kissed Steven on the cheek, then turned to his Aunt and greeted her. "Hello, Mrs. Prentice-Hall...Molly. You look enchanting this evening."

"Thank you my dear, and you look chic and magnificent as always, Mrs. Prentice-Hall replied. "What can we get you to drink before we all sit for dinner?"

"Sure, I would love a martini."

Francine took a seat next to Steven and turned to ask, "How was your day?"

Within moments of asking, a fabulously chilled martini appeared. Francine accepted the glass and immediately took a sip. The moment the cool liquid touched her lips and spilled through her mouth, her tone instantly reset and she went into a more relaxed mode. She could now exhale, free from worry that she was needed to tend to a garment or answer a needed question.

Steven reached over to put his arm around the back of the cushion, creating a connected union, a proper public connection. "Aunt Molly wants to know how the the wedding plans are going."

"Well, the dress has been started, but Steven we still have a lot of planning to discuss."

"I hope that you both don't mind, I would love to offer you both help with the planning," Aunt Molly interjected "In fact, if you both haven't decided on a location for your guests after the church. I wanted to offer you both the option of the country club or my home as possible choices, depending on the amount of guests that you would like to invite?"

"Those are both wonderful options," Steven said. "What

do you think, Francine?"

"I agree, I think that they're both incredible options, I feel so privileged to be even offered them. How about Steven and I talk about it and we will get back to you with what option would be better for us?"

Aunt Molly nodded, then quickly added, "Don't worry about the invitations either, we will have the family printer take care of everything, and of course add the family crest."

"Wow, this is amazing...thank you so much." Francine pivots towards Steven in excitement, "Steven let's talk soon about more specifics so that we can get back to your Aunt with our choices."

Steven leaned towards Francine and replied, "Absolutely!"

"Well, lets go in for dinner now," Aunt Molly said. "I don't know about you both, but I'm starving." Everyone stood, Steven waited for the ladies to pass through the main rooms, as he allowed them to enter the dining room first. He went immediately to his Aunt's chair and pulled out her chair first, and then proceeded next to assist Francine with her chair. Francine admired the table with its white linen tablecloth and napkins which created the perfect backdrop of softness against the cool white china. The china is adorned with Prentice-Hall family crest, along with the added touch of a rim of gold along all of the edges. The flowers, the china, and the sterling silver serving pieces were the finest available creating one magnificent table presentation. The room was finished off with a exquisite set of silk drapes that complimented not only the classic simple damask wallpaper print, but the beautiful art collection that the Prentice-Hall family collected from around the world.

Aunt Molly, proposes the first toast to open the meal, "To Steven and Molly, may you know many years of bliss, health and prosperity."

They clinked their glasses together, creating a delicate chime for that proper closure to her good wishes. Aunt Molly signaled the wait staff to present the plated dishes to the table for their dinner. Both Steven and Aunt Molly, enjoyed their food, obvious by the sounds coming from them both. Francine on the other hand was silent, barely picking at her food.

Aunt Molly glanced up from her plate, "Francine, is everything okay with your food?"

"Oh yes, it's wonderful. My stomach seems to be a little sensitive today, but everything is simply delicious."

"Please, let me get you something else," Molly offered, "perhaps something a little less heavy?"

"No...really I'm fine, I'm sure it's just nerves!"

Uncomfortable, Francine decided to make more of an

effort to eat. She glanced over at Steven as he just shoveled it down. When he noticed her looking at him, he smiled back and slowed down. Francine broke the nervous energy with a soft clearing of her throat and said, "I feel like I finally settled on a design for my wedding gown."

"Oh, how wonderful." As Molly places her fork down and clasps her hands together, "I need to take some time to stop by the shop to see it."

Francine nodded and smiled. "Please, I would love that,"

"Me too," Steven agreed, and then he laughed.

They finished with dinner, and proceeded back to the main sitting area for after dinner cocktails.

"I know that both of you need more time to review a guest list, but if you had to select now, which way do you think that you would lean?" Molly asked.

"Well, I think the country club would be the best option," Steven said.

"Me too." Francine agreed. "Presuming that it will be at least close to hundred, if not over. It would be the best for all if we just have it at the club."

"Yes," Steven seconded. "Aunt Molly as beautiful as your home is, I would be devastated if something was broken or damaged."

"I understand, just let me know whatever you both decide," Molly said.

"Where are you both thinking about going on your honeymoon?"

"We really didn't get that far into the planning stage yet." Steven responded.

"Another thing to consider," Molly suggested, "Is my *pied-a-terre* on *Cote d' Azur.*

"Molly, your generosity has been more than Steven and I could ever repay or thank you for," gushes Francine.

"Nonsense my dear. Please, it's available for both of you. The place just sits there. I'm getting to old and tired to do that ocean cruise anymore. Francine, it's perfect for you both, and plus you haven't been back to your homeland since you have arrived. It's time!"

Over-whelmed with gratitude, Francine broke down and started crying.

"Please don't cry my child, I didn't mean to upset you." As Molly got up to console Francine.

"No really you didn't...I'm just so over-whelmed." Embarrassed Francine ran from the room.

Steven stood up to follow, then stopped.

"Steven, leave her," Aunt Molly said as she walked back to her favorite chair, "She needs a moment."

"Aunt Molly I just think she is tired, and overwhelmed

by everything. All of these opportunities being presented to her are situations that her family would never be able to offer to her."

"I know my dear, but I hope that I haven't over stepped."

"No, no. Not at all. It's just a lot for her to take in. They're simple people, they arrived here with practically nothing."

"Yes," Aunt Molly responds in a hushed tone.

Steven and Aunt Molly waited in silence. Not an uncomfortable silence, but one of solidarity. When Francine returned Steven stood up and immediately walked over to her. He proceeded to ask Francine how she is doing, and she responded in a brisk tone, "I'm fine, Steven, but I think that is time for me to say good-night. Darling will you please forgive me, and walk me to my car?"

"Of course," Steve said.

Francine squatted down next to Aunt Molly's chair, "Molly, I need to apologize for my outburst, but of course thank you for your extreme generosity. This is really something I'm not used to, but, believe me when I say that my heart is so full." Francine's eyes filled with tears and her voice cracked as she spoke the words.

Aunt Molly reached out to touch Francine's hand. While she gently grasped her hand she stated, "Good-night my dear, you're family now, what's mine is yours. I will be here waiting to hear what Steven and you decide."

Steven helped Francine up, and guided her towards the main entrance of the home. He opened the front door for her and they continued down the front walkway, the very same walkway where she first laid eyes on Steven. Now here she was, a business woman and about to be his wife. It had all happened so fast.

The coolness of the night helped to calm Francine.

"Francine, I just want you to know that I understand," Steven said as he'd open the car door for Francine. "There have been so many changes occurring in your life, in such a short period of time."

"I was thinking that too my love. Not that these things are bad, oh my gosh no! All of these opportunities have been truly wonderful. It's just been very overwhelming, having so much being offered and so suddenly."

Steven leaned in and hugged Francine.

"Oh, Steven that feels so good. How do you always know actually what I need? Hold me tighter, it feels so comforting. Something about your arms around me, gives me the feeling that I'm safe."

"I'm glad." Steven said, "but most of all I'm glad you're in my life, I love you."

"I love you too," Francine took Steven's face in her hands and reached in to kiss him gently, so soft, so tender.

Steven responded by taking it a little further and a touch harder, careful not to push it to far. He wanted her to know that he was there for her but also understood that she needs her space too. A silent dialogue shared only by those with the deepest of connections. One that delineates all time.

As Francine was carefully placed into her drivers seat. She rolled the window down and started the car, "Steven, you will always be my everything."

Steven reached in through the window, "And you're mine, please drive home safe, I will talk to you tomorrow."

Francine smiled up at him. "Okay, tomorrow."

With that good-bye, Francine pulled out of the long curved driveway and onto the street.

Steven watched the tail lights until they completely disappeared.

As Francine drove away she became lost in the blur of stoplights, headlights and thoughts, trying to understand her discomfort. It wasn't Steven, he was the love of her life. Nor was it her business. Perhaps Aunt Molly was correct it was everything hitting her all at once. Running a business, planning a wedding and becoming a home owner. Her life had been so simple and quiet before. Now it's all about planning, appointments and timelines. Did she rush into making this grand party when all she needed was an intimate celebration of love.

The oncoming headlights burned her eye's like spotlights, Francine tired to squint to dim the intensity of the oncoming beams. But the beams seem to grow as she struggled to see. All while emotions forced through her like a river that could not be stopped.

Chapter Twenty:
Another Day at Work?

Steven arrived at his place of work, the family's publishing house. A stone tower of classic architecture with it's stone gargoyles in all corners, sitting their for decades in allegiance to form some sort of protection. He quickly worked his way up to the 10th floor, as he passes the secretaries with the typewriter's all screaming in some sort of off tempo beat. He finally approached his office door, and just as he pulls the door open his personal secretary hands him a healthy pile of messages. Steven then proceeded through the final door on his daily journey, to discover his desk still quietly awaits him.

Taking his usual position behind a desk that has a placard stating, Vice-President. Steven decided to ignore the messages and call Francine instead. He wanted to make sure that she was doing better today. Before the first ring was even completed, Peggy, Francine's assistant, answered. After the usual greeting, Peggy stated, that Francine had not arrived yet. But, as soon as she does, she would let her know right away that I've called.

They hung up and Steven decided to call his Aunt. This time it seemed like an eternity of rings, before one of the servants finally picked up the line.

"Prentice-Hall residence."

"Hello, this is Steven is my Aunt available?"

"Yes, one moment and I will get her for you."

Minutes ticked by like hours, Mrs. Prentice-Hall doesn't hurry for anyone. Finally his Aunt picked up the phone.

"Hello, Steven?"

"Hello, how are you doing?

"Well, thank you. What is the reason for your call this morning?"

"I just wanted to say thank you again for everything that you have offered us in preparation for the wedding. The choice of your home or the country club, and then your place in France for the honeymoon. Just the thought of Francine being able to return home on our honeymoon was just a little to much to handle for her at that point."

"Oh, I completely understand, how is she doing today?" Aunt Molly asked.

"I'm sure she is fine, I will be speaking with her sometime today. I will let you know everything we discuss when we have dinner tomorrow on Saturday. I'm pretty sure that we're both leaning towards the country club and of course staying at your place in France, for sure. I will give you a call in a couple of days and we can talk more about it."

"Okay I'll will look forward to hearing from you soon."

With that Steven and Aunt Molly both hung up the phone.

As Steven placed the phone receiver back into the cradle, his sleeve brushed the pile of messages still waiting to be read. The messages now strewn across his desk as he spun around to look out the floor to ceiling glass window. As he closes his eyes, something jolted his memory and without hesitation he turned back around and faced his desk. Remembering that he'd seen the name Dubois written several times on those pieces of paper that now decorate his desk top.

Steven grabbed the messages and chaotically thumbed through them. Each time he noticed a message with the name Dubois on it, he placed it aside. By the time he'd finished the pile he found three. All delivered within the hour before he'd arrived. Steven then jumped up and left his office to speak with his secretary.

"Janet, can you tell me who left these messages, it just says Dubois?"

"Yes?" she replied.

"Well? Steven pressed. "Was it Francine?"

"Oh no, an older woman called the first two times and

then it was an older man."

"Okay, thanks."

Steven ran back to his desk and dialed the Dubois home. The phone rang and rang, but no one is picked up. Steven then proceeded to call the Francine again at her shop.

Peggy picked up. "Francine Dubois's office how may I help you?"

"Hi Peggy, it's Steven again did Francine get in yet?"

"No, not yet." Peggy replied.

"Okay, please have her call me the moment that she walks in the door."

"Absolutely."

Steven hung up the phone with Peggy, and redialed the Dubois', still no answer. Steven got up from his desk and walked over to the large glass window.

As he scanned the city, he tried to focus on the beauty of the view, but his mind wouldn't allow the distraction. Overcome by an instinctual feeling that his Chicago skyline was not reflecting back the same excitement and wondrous possibilities that it once had, just moments ago.

It felt harsh, cold, and it was the middle of summer. The steel structures of strength now haunted him. His reflection in the glass feels vapid, while he glanced over a city that he loved and loved him back. But, now a cold sobering fact hits him that all of life was a reflection of self, and he did not like what was staring back at him.

The more Steven thought, the more agitated he became. So much so, that he needed to leave. As he bolted out of his office, Steven told his secretary, "I'm leaving for the day. If Francine or the Dubois' call again, please call my Aunt's home and leave a message for me there."

"Will do!" she replied briskly.

Frustrated, with the fact that he couldn't get a hold of Francine, compounded with this strange feeling coming over him, Steven needed to be reassured that all was okay.

Steven worked his way back down the elevator, past the guard and back out through the revolving door again. Still lost in his repetitive thought pattern, he wound his way towards the lot where he'd parked. His imagination of everything that could have happened could fill the parking lot that he was now in, ten times over. He knew that he might have been overacting but he didn't care. Why would he receive so many messages from the Dubois' in such a short period of time? Whether his concerns were justified or not, Steven rationalized that this would be just another opportunity to physically see Francine before tomorrow. So, in his mind this would be a win-win either way.

Steven made the long trip up Lake Shore Drive, heading to the northern suburbs. The drive north along the water calmed Steven. Thirty minutes later, he finally arrived at

Francine's studio and immediately noticed that her car was not there. He debated whether he should run in, or go straight the Dubois' home. Thinking that he would hate to drive all the way back to the shop on a technicality, so Steven quickly threw the car in a parking place in front of the shop and ran in. Taking several stairs at once, as he made his way to Francine's office until he was finally face to face with Peggy, "Has Francine arrived yet?"

"No," Peggy said, "in fact it's kind of strange because she is usually here by now?"

Steven didn't reply, he just turned and left. As Steven hurried back to his car, his mind raced. Had she gotten cold feet and needed some distance for a while? Was all of this way too much and too soon? Steven hoped he hadn't scared Francine off.

His body was in the car, holding the steering wheel as he made the drive to the Dubios', but his mind was a million miles away. He gripped the steering wheel harder, almost as though he was trying to will his mind back to the car, so he didn't think of anything negative. Why would she leave? They could always postpone the wedding. Hell, if she wanted they could even elope. He just wanted her to understand that they could take this as a slow as she would like. As Steven continued the mental debate of rationalizing his greatest fear, Steven finally arrived at the Dubois' home.

Steven pulled into the driveway, concentrating on willing her presence in the house. Fantasizing that he now sees Francine peering out the window, waving and then running out the door to greet him.

But nothing.

He worked his way to the door and rang the bell. The door opened onto Mr. Dubois. Steven found that strange. He thought that for sure that both Mr. Dubois and his wife would he at the tailor shop, especially on a Friday afternoon. An eerie stoicism radiated from Mr. Dubois as he opened the screen door and stepped aside to allow Steven to cross the threshold. There he finds Mrs. Dubois sitting on the sofa, crying.

Steven immediately walked to her side, "What's wrong? Why are you crying?"

"Francine, Francine." Noelle screamed through her tears.

"What about her? Steven asked. "Did she run away? She's probably scared, everything has been happening so fast. Perhaps it's all too much for her right now. Don't worry Mrs. Dubois, I will find her."

Mr. Dubois reached over to touch Steven on the shoulder, "No, Steven you can't bring her home."

Steven's brows furrowed, "Sure I can, she's just a little over stressed right now with all the wedding plans, the new home and news about our honeymoon. Did you know we're going back to France for our honeymoon?"

Noelle cried even harder now, wailing, "Oh my Francine, my baby she's gone."

"I know, but that's what I'm trying to tell you," Steven persisted, "I will find her and bring her home."

Mr. Dubois took Steven by the arms, raised him off the sofa and looked him dead in the eyes. Steven noticed that Mr. Dubois had tears in his eyes. "No Steven, Francine can't come home. She is dead. She was killed last night, in a car crash."

Steven fell back down on the sofa, "What? That's impossible. That can't be true."

The room was now frozen in time, no existence outside of these four walls that surrounded them. They were stuck, collapsing in the memories of what was, while trying to understand their new reality. Steven's mind went wild with denial as they all tried to console each other. The deafening stillness of sadness filled the home.

"How could someone so loved and so full of life...be gone?" Steven asked.

Mr. and Mrs. Dubois broke down again.

Steven sat motionless staring out the window, too scared to move or react as though movement would somehow validate that this whole horrible situation was real.

Chapter Twenty-One: The Dance

A black dress swayed slightly from the breeze coming from the open window as it hung in the doorway. It wasn't just any dress, it was the dress that Dallas had finally selected – or maybe best to say that Alex happened to stumble upon. As Dallas approached the hanging dress and double checked it for wrinkles. Dallas also noticed that a text had just arrived from Alex, stating that she was on her way over to the house, so that they both could get ready together.

Dallas sat at her vanity and pushed around her make-up brushes as she tried to select from the numerous color palettes of eye shadows. She wanted to make sure that the one she selected was the right choice for this evening. Dallas usually preferred to wear a limited amount of make-up, but tonight was a special occasion so she needed to take a little extra time.

Another text arrived from Alex, saying that she was pulling up in the driveway, so Dallas screamed to let anyone downstairs know that Alex was here and to please let her in.

Within minutes Dallas heard the echo of Alex's foot-steps as she worked her way up the stairs. Dallas knew the sound so well that she could tell what flight someone was on just by the sound of the squeak. "Hey girl." Dallas shouted, moments before Alex pushed her door open.

Alex pushed the door open, this routine was so com-mon for her now that the mere fact that Dallas always seemed to know the precise moment that she would push the door open, no longer fazed her.

"Hey back," Alex said, "How's it going?"

"Just trying to figure out what is the best shade to wear."

"Cool...we have lots of time yet, no hurry."

Alex plopped herself down on the bed and started ham-mering away on her phone. "Did you talk to Zach yet?"

"No," Dallas replied. "How about Josh?"

"Yeah. The guys will get here around 7:00. But, when I was talking to Josh, Zach still hadn't arrived at Josh's place yet."

"I didn't think he would be there yet anyways, guys are so last minute."

"So true!"

Dallas changed the subject, "Have you been to that restaurant that we're going to tonight-before? You know, with your parents, or Josh?"

"No," Alex said, "first time for me, how about you?"

"No, but my parents have been there with my Grandpa, in fact I heard it's one of his favorites. He's coming by tonight too."

"Really?"

"Yeah...mom always likes to parade me in front of family-when I'm all fancy."

Alex cracked a smirk, "Been there. I haven't seen your Grandpa in quite a while, it will be really good to see him again."

"Yeah, he used to come around a lot, but my Dad said that he shouldn't really be driving any more. He hated that, so my Dad got him a driver."

Dallas and her grandfather had been close for many years, especially when she was a child. By the time Dallas turned 8, her grandfather had been well into retirement and was looking to spend more time with family; they'd just clicked. Around the age of 12 Dallas's grandfather started taking her on trips around the world. Morocco, France, Italy, even Bali were some of the stamps they had collected on their passports.

Sometimes we try to understand how the synchronicity of people occurs. Yes, he was Dallas's Grandfather, but it was more than that. The connection between the two was never like a forced family gathering or imposition. Her grandfather to Dallas, was just someone that she liked hang out with and enjoyed talking with. His age was never a factor, in fact Dallas usually tired out well before he did when traveling and discovering exotic locations.

But as Dallas got older, girlfriends and boys soon took the priority. But that connection would always be there between the two of them, no matter how time went by and how separate their individual lives had become.

The girls stopped chatting and turned the music up as a signal that they needed to get heavy into the "getting ready" process. Because the only thing that really mattered was the big reveal to their dates. They started with make-up, then they helped each other with their hair. Last came dresses, shoes, and accessories, then they were out the door.

"Shit!" Dallas shouted when the doorbell rang.

Both of the girls went into hyper drive. In fact, they both started running into each other because they were both trying to rush and locate everything they needed for the night.

"Charger?" Alex practically screamed.

"Got it!" Dallas fired back.

"Okay...now let the unveiling begin."

Both Dallas and Alex hurried out the bedroom door and started the long descent down the stairs slowly in heels, to make their grand entrance. At the bottom of stairs, Dallas immediately noticed that they had quite an audience waiting for them at the bottom. Alex arrived first and went to Josh's side. Dallas took a moment for a poetic pause on the fourth step from the bottom, cognitive of drawing her audience in. Dallas really knew how to dress and pull outfits together that had a unique look and style that's all her own. Her dress was deep emerald green taffeta that matched her eyes beautifully. It fell to mid-calf length with an outer attached layer that was longer in the back, a large portrait collar bodice, and three quarter length sleeve. The dress looked like it was custom made for her petite frame, all cut on the bias tightly cinched at waist with darts, and finished off with self-covered buttons that ran up the front of the bodice.

The faces of Dallas' parents and grandfather were full of smiles. Dallas walked over to hug her grandpa, her mom, and then her dad.

"Wow, this is kind of awkward everybody is just staring," she said.

"You look so beautiful Dallas," Mom stated, then she proceeded to document the moment by taking pictures, lots and lots of pictures. Their dates handed them their flowers, then even more pictures. A few minutes later,

Dallas's grandfather suddenly shouted, "Wait. Dallas you have a label or something hanging out of the back of your dress on the collar?"

Her grandpa walked over to Dallas and reached over to adjust the back of her dress. Suddenly, he froze, her grandpa seriously tensed up and he then immediately started to back up.

"Grandpa what's wrong?"

Dallas' Dad walked to his side when Grandpa didn't repsond.

"Dad, what is it? Are you okay?" Dallas' Dad stated nervously.

"Grandpa what's wrong?" Dallas repeated.

Dallas was about to ask what was wrong a third time when her Dad said:

"Dallas help me get him to a chair so he can sit down."

Dallas and her dad walked her grandfather over to the chair. He was as white as a ghost. Immediately, Dallas' mom ran to the kitchen to get some water.

"Dad, what's wrong can you tell me? Dallas' Dad asked. "Are you in pain?"

"Grandpa, I'm worried," Dallas said, "I don't want to leave unless I know that you're okay."

They gathered around the chair that he'd been lowered into and stared at him. Waiting for any kind of acknowledgment to reassure them that he was okay until he finally broke his silence. "Dallas, I'm okay. Really. You need to go the dance. I was just stunned for a moment, but I'm fine."

Dallas wasn't 100% comfortable about leaving, but she knew that he would be in safe hands. So, everyone going to the dance re-positioned themselves outside, in order take some of the attention from her grandfather, "Okay let's take a couple of more pictures outside and then we really should get to the restaurant. But, before we do, grandpa you have to promise me that you're fine?"

"Yes, Dallas really I'm fine. Go, have a great time, I want to hear all about your evening tomorrow. I will be staying the night, so we will have a lot to talk about tomorrow."

"Are you sure?" Dallas asked.

"Yes, very!"

Dallas and everybody resumed taking some more pictures before they all left for the restaurant. As everybody moved outside, grandpa stayed inside sitting, still in shock. After about thirty minutes of goodbyes and constant waving of arms and hands "goodbye," Dallas's parents returned inside the home.

"Dad, you gave us all a scare there for a minute Are you

really okay? Or were you just saying that so that Dallas wouldn't be scared?" Dallas' Dad stated.

"No," Grandpa replied, "I actually really was just more stunned than anything."

"Stunned?" Dallas' Dad interjected.

"Yes."

"Stunned from what?" Dallas' Dad continued.

"Well, that's a really long story." Grandpa stated.

"Were not going anywhere," Dallas's Dad replied, "and it's the perfect night for a long conversation."

"Wow, I don't even know where to start?" Grandpa sighed.

"At the beginning...of course." His son replied.

"I'm sure that is the most logical, but these are memories that I buried along time along. As Grandpa continued, almost seeming agitated. "I don't know how many of those memories I want to relive and shake up."

"I understand, but now you have me curious on what stirred up such deep emotions." Dallas' Dad insisted.

"Okay, well I see dinner is coming out, so why don't I go upstairs and wash up and I will be down and seated at the table in a short time." As Grandpa worked his way out of the chair.

"Sounds good." His son said, almost sounding reassured.

Steven made his way upstairs, navigating the same stairs that he had taken thousands of times before. He made it all the way up the three fights. He wanted to see the secret room again. The room that held a special memory for Francine and him. He pushed the door open to find it so much different from what he remembered and the original vision and experience that he'd had. But that's what happens welcomed or not, life changes.

He finds the secret room, now filled with collected pieces of memories of the past. Fused together in a vision that was now Dallas's. Steven felt the love that Dallas had put in the space, and he thought of how Francine would have enjoyed it too. Steven walked up to the large window overlooking the lake, and found himself lost in the memories, while captured by the beauty of what is.

Remembering that he was needed downstairs, he worked his way back down the stairs carrying that love energy with him. Almost as though he was needing to reconnect to that memory so that he could find the courage to tell a long forgotten story of love.

Chapter Twenty-Two: Candlelight Dinner with a Side of Wonderful Memories!

The dishes were being collected off the table while the desserts and the appropriate beverages for the final course were poured and served. Mom and Dad were hanging on to every word that Grandpa Steven was sharing about his incredible story of a past love.

"Dad, wait...before you finish...what about mom?" Dallas's Dad stated.

"What about her?" Grandpa Steven asked. "I loved her very much, I just happened to meet Francine first. So now where did I leave off? Oh...yeah."

"The afternoon that I went over to the Dubois' home, was a day that shifted my whole life obviously. I was devastated and destroyed and it took me a long time to work through the loss of Francine. In fact, this very house, I bought it for her. I stayed here because it was my last remaining connection to her."

The look on Steven's son's face dropped, but Steven didn't care. These were Steven's life choices, it had nothing to do with him.

Steven continued on, "So the Dubois's needed to go and identify the body. I offered to take them, of course. I wanted to honor Francine and make sure that everything was taken care of. It was horrible seeing Francine's body bruised and cold. That memory still haunts me.

They never paid for anything, I took care of all of the expenses and handled all of the arrangements. I made sure that she had the best of everything. I wanted the world to know that it had lost someone very special.

The Dubois' and I remained close until Mrs. Dubois's death about 10 years Francine's death, perhaps from a broken heart. They were very close. I heard Mr. Dubois, tried to keep the shop going after her death, but there really was no reason. Everyone that was important in his life, was now gone. The last thing I heard, that Mr. Dubois sold the family home, closed the shop and went back to France. I never heard from him again. I just think that the memories were just too painful for him here."

His son clung on to every last detail of his story, "Dad, what happened to Francine's shop?"

"It stayed open for about three months after Francine's

death just to finish up all of the client's orders. But there was no life, no energy in the shop of course. Francine's vision and spirit were what drove that shop. They were just trying to get things completed so that they too could move on.

In the last days your Great Aunt Molly and myself sold off a lot of the machinery. Daily, I would do my usual walk through making sure all of the elements that needed to be removed, were.

Eventually, I needed to find enough courage to work my way up to her office. I proceeded up the main staircase, with a heaviness almost to much to bare. That heaviness was from knowing that Francine would not be on the other side of her office door. I had pretty much left her office for last. Maybe because I knew it might be the most difficult. I opened the door and immediately lost my breath. There it was, in the middle of the room, "The Dress." Someone had placed her wedding dress in there for safe-keeping. Perhaps, because no one knew just what to do with it. It was the most beautiful thing I had ever seen...besides Francine of course. The seamstresses went ahead and finished it. Every detail was perfect and looked just like her sketches. I needed to just sit, and take in the beauty of that dress and embrace my reality. The reality was that I would never see her in that dress, nor would she ever be truly mine again.

So, when I saw the label on the back of Dallas's dress, all of those memories came flooding back. Memories that I thought that I packed away neatly so long ago. The dress that Dallas was wearing tonight was from one of her collections."

"Wow," as both Steven's son and daughter-in-law both simultaneously sighed.

"That was probably one of the most amazing stories I think I ever heard." Dallas's mom leaned back in her chair, while also wiping tears from her eyes.

Dallas's Dad looked shocked, as though he'd just found out his whole life was a lie. Somehow, he felt cheated that his mom was not "the one."

Steven sensed his son's disillusion, but he knew that he'd loved his mother too. Maybe it wasn't the same, but it didn't make it any less real. Dallas' mom was the opposite she was glowing from the essence of love that was pouring out from his story, and the presence of that energy that now engulfed the room as he talked of such a deep connection.

Chapter Twenty-Three: The True Secret Room!

The family was sitting around the table in the breakfast room when Dallas wandered in blurry-eyed.

"Well, good afternoon!" Dallas' Dad chimed in first.

Mom followed Dad's snarky comment, "Stop. Dallas didn't get up that late. Besides she had a good excuse to sleep in a little."

"Good morning everybody," Dallas replied.

A round of "Good Mornings," rang back to Dallas.

"I had such a good time last night," Dallas said, "but before I go into everything that happened at the dance last night, Grandpa...I need to know what happened to you?"

Her mom jumped in, "Oh my gosh, Dallas you will never believe the story behind the dress that you wore last night. Seriously!"

Dallas raised a brow. "Really? What? Tell me."

"Grandpa told us the whole story last night, it was amazing." Dallas' Mom stated with excitement.

"No way, come on," Dallas sat in the chair beside her Dad, "inquiring minds need to know."

"First, you tell us about last night." Steven interjected.

Dallas, now wide-eyed with excitement about getting center stage to talk about her amazing night at the dance. "Oh my gosh guys, it was the best night ever. First, we went to this amazing restaurant, then of course we all went to the dance, and after that we all headed to the beach for a bonfire. It was magical, I really like Zach a lot.

"Wow, I'm so glad that you had a good time and that you really like Zach." Mom stated.

"I agree with your Mom completely." Her Dad quickly added.

Dallas now turns her face towards Grandpa. "Okay, Grandpa now spill it, why did you freak out last night when you fixed the back of my dress?"

"Wow, I need to spill it?" Grandpa leans back in the chair almost as though the words verbally knocked him back. "Okay, how about this, why don't you and I go for a drive and I will tell you all about, 'the dress' that you wore last night."

Dallas nodded. "Okay, I will run upstairs and grab a shower and change, how about we meet downstairs in about 30 minutes."

"Sounds good," Steven agreed.

Both Steven and Dallas excused themselves from the breakfast table. As Dallas ran up the stairs to her bedroom on the second floor to shower and change, her grandfather worked his way upstairs to the third floor, but this time instead of heading to Dallas's hideaway...he went just a little beyond it.

Steven ran his fingers under the wood trim as he felt his way along the wood paneling, until he reached a metal latch. He then pressed that latch and a part of the paneling proceeded to pop open. Steven then took his fingers and pulled the side of the paneling that popped open, which now clearly formed a doorway. Pulling the door completely open, Steven stepped into the true "secret room."

There was no light in the room so Steven reached for the wall switch and a simple ceiling light immediately illuminated what had once been a small dark space, into a presence. A presence of a beautiful dress on a simple dress form. The light allowed it to come alive once again, as the sequins that Francine's staff so lovingly sewn on one-by-one bounced light prisms onto the walls. It was almost as magical as the woman that was meant to wear it.

The white dress stood as a tribute throughout time, in it's own private space, as a dedication to a love so deep that time could not erase it.